Prelude

All I remember is the cold pod. I do not even know if I had any parents to begin with. After the pod, "The Facility" as some of the workers called it, was our new home. We would have to go through a multitude of tests and injections to perfect us. Mother always explained that we are different from other humans: the Lessers. We are smarter and stronger than the average humans. we are EVOs. Mother told us that when the time was right, we would be sent out to shake the world and that the only people we should stay away from are the Novas and the Teltius. She taught us that Novas are the only humans that could match our strength and that we would be able to tell them apart from the rest, because they always have two different eye colors. While a Teltius isn't as strong as us, they have no equals when it came to their intellects, and their silver eyes are what stood them apart from the Lessers.

Our days were always the same: studying to be better than we were meant to be; training our bodies to be stronger, faster, and more deadly. She taught us the act of killing by having us kill one another's pets. We each had our own pet. Mine was a bird while Maxwell had a turtle. We slept with them and lived with them until we were forced to kill them. We did this over and over until our eyes were dead.

I remember the first time we met a Lesser, we could not have been older than thirteen. Mother walked into class announcing the start of a new lesson and a fun task. She then walked out only to come back a few minutes later with a tied up and blindfolded, scared man. The Lesser walked in accompanied by a smell so dreadful that we felt sick to our stomachs. Some of us even threw up; I remember the taste of my vomit until this day. The odor was so bad that we begged Mother to get rid of it. Mother then called the help to take the blindfolded man out, and just like magic, once he was taken out, the smell disappeared. While we recuperated, Mother began to explain.

"That was a Lesser. You are not one of them, because you have all been created to be the next evolutionary step of humanity. Evolution has made you the predator of these weak humans. Your goal is eradication. You will learn to endure the smell because, you will

2

experience a kill like no other. A kill so blissful and euphoric that you will forget that smell even existed." She walked around the room with a smile. "Now, go clean up, and we will try this again."

We all got up and left the room to go clean ourselves. For the first time, we felt weak which was something we hated. We wanted to remove this foreign enemy called the Lesser. When we were back in the classroom, I could see from each of our eyes that there was no question of what was going to happen next. We welcomed it because weakness is not a part of us.

Mother gleamed with delight. "The look in your eyes does not disappoint me. You already know what is to come. You will have your first kill today this will be your first step at eliminating the Lessers. I will bring him back in and this time there's only one way he will leave when the exercise is over."

The help brought the Lesser into the classroom and as soon as he did, the smell came back—but this time, none of us threw up. We didn't want to feel that weakness ever again. Another helper came and put a knife on the desk in front of every one of us and we knew what had to be done, no crying or hesitation. Before Mother said anything more, Luther walked up knife in hand to the blindfolded man. We all began getting up and following Luther's steps. When he got close to the blindfolded man, he stopped and without hesitation we joined him, forming a circle around the man. Tears ran down our cheeks—not because we were scared, but because the smell had gotten stronger. Luther was smiling, and so were my other brothers and sisters. We were all smiling from seeing that man squirm. He didn't know where he was. He was scared and for some reason that excited us—a Lesser that stood in our presence without knowing who he was in front of. Mother had told us that we would be killing Lessers in the future and now the time had come to kill our first one.

Luther walked closer to the man, saying, "It is going to be alright."

When the man calmed down a bit Luther took advantage, slashing the man's arm. The man screamed and tried to escape, but Michelle grabbed his shirt and with a grin asked, "Where are you going?" while sliding her knife into his lower back. We could smell it for the first time, a smell that sent electricity through our brains while canceling out the bad smell. Have you ever smelled something that just made you stop in your tracks and feel like the only person in existence? We all rushed him and started stabbing. With every pull, a gush of blood followed, and every stab released the amazing aroma.

"Enough!" Mother commanded. "I told you we were going to have fun, and did you?"

"Yes, mother!" We cheered.

"Now that you know the smell of death, I will teach you how to survive and blend with the Lessers."

That was the day we truly realized that we were EVOs.

Chapter 1

The alarm buzzed at 5:00AM as Richard stretched his hand and lazily hit the snooze button. He got kicked hard by his lover, upset. Richard turned around to face him.

"What the hell was that for? I'm trying to get some extra sleep here."

"If you set the alarm for 5:00 in the morning to supposedly go to the gym and don't go, I'm going to murder you," Marc grumbled.

"In my defense, I thought I needed to go to the gym before going to bed, but when I woke up I realized this sweet body is already shredded," Richard joked.

"Please, whatever you tell yourself. Just remember if this alarm goes off again without you getting out of bed, you will leave in a body bag."

"Well, excuse me, as I get out of bed."

"That's what I thought."

Richard got up and randomly picked his clothes in the darkness as not to disturb Marc. He navigated to the bathroom, brushed his teeth and splashed some water on his face as he stared at his reflection. "Still look handsome," he said as he passed his hand through his thick hair. He went to the dining room and got dressed as he listened to the news playing in the background. He went to the kitchen to feed the cats who were swarming his leg, meowing. The second he opened a can of food, one of the cats jumped on the counter.

"Shoo, shoo, not on the counter. We are civilized here."

He poured the cat food in three bowls and proceeded to carry all three while trying not to step on the cats swarming around him. After feeding the girls, he went to clean their litter box.

By six he was sitting down with a fresh cup of overly sweet, watching the news, until 7:00 when Marc got up.

"How was the gym?" Marc inquired.

Richard smiled smugly. "About that."

"You didn't go."

"Well, I had to take care of these beautiful creatures we have in the apartment."

Marc walked to their coffee station. "You didn't even make me coffee!"

"Sorry. I fired the maid this morning—but you could make your own coffee."

"The way you act sometimes, nobody would ever picture you as one of the best detectives in the force."

"I'm one of the best because I see the bigger picture."

"Funny, I thought it was because of Alice." Marc smirked.

Richard paused. "Every serial killer is different yet the same—there's an urge that pushes them to do the taboo. They always try to create a puzzle that cannot be solved, but I always solve it, and that's the fun part. But Alice does help a little. Just a bit!"

"Maybe I should write a piece about you and Alice and name it *Who Can Outwit the Greatest Detectives*"

Richard leaned in and whispered "Wouldn't that be fun? Just make sure to use my name in the title." He kissed Marc.

"Hey, unlike you, I need to finish getting ready."

By 8:00 AM Marc was done and ready to leave and so was Richard. They both left their apartment together.

Richard pulled out his car keys. "Do you need a ride?"

"So you can pick me up late again? No, thank you."

"That was one time." Richard winced.

"Actually, twice. You forgot to pick me up twice."

"What I'm hearing is that third time's the charm." Richard smiled.

"Nope. There's no third time."

"Alright, I guess I'll see you tonight," Richard said as he kissed Marc goodbye.

"Unless you come home late."

"Touché."

Richard took his usual route, parking by the small coffee shop by his job for his caramel latte with extra caramel.

"I would like a caramel latte," Richard said to the barista.

"With extra caramel, right?" The barista replied.

"Okay, I come here too often—but yes to the extra caramel—and with an extra shot of espresso in there, please."

"So this is your 10th order, I'm assuming, since you only do the espresso shot with your free order."

"You know it." Richard smiled.

"Here you go! Extra caramel and a shot of espresso," the barista said.

"Thank you." Richard took a sip, tasting the caramel and the espresso combined.

"This is heaven," Richard whispered. "Okay, time for work."

Richard took his time walking to work while enjoying his coffee and the morning breeze. He threw the empty cup in the trash, walked up the small stairs, and stepped into a day he couldn't see coming.

A couple of hours prior, Alice was at the gym looking at her watch.

"That little shit isn't coming. Is he?" Alice said to herself. "And I was thinking of going easy on him today." Thinking of what she would do to him during their next workout together left her smiling.

"Told you he wasn't going to come," her friend replied.

"Well, good thing I have you." Alice laughed.

After an hour of working out, Alice headed back home where her husband had already made breakfast.

"Something smells good," Alice said as she kissed Phillip.

"It will smell better after you take a shower."

"You don't have to tell me twice." Alice said as she went to shower and change into her work outfit.

"Coffee?"

"Sure." She took a seat as the news played in the background. All the while rubbing her temple.

"I take it that Richard was a no show this morning?" Phillip said, trying to hold back his smile.

"What gave you that impression?"

"The fact that you only rub your temple when you are annoyed, but I prefer to think of it as husband's intuition." They both laughed as they started eating.

"So, anything interesting happening in the news?" She asked.

"We're still fighting in a war, the mayoral election is about to start, and we might have a Nova running. Oh! There's been rumors of Darius being on the move."

"If he's on the move, then the Teltius peoples must also be moving."

"They don't even care. They don't see us or the people of Menea as equal. At least the Menean put their life on the line instead of just sitting behind their fortress." Phillip saw the frown on Alice's face and stopped. "Sorry."

"It's okay, I get why you're angry and you should be. I love it when you express yourself," Alice said, grabbing his hand.

"How do you like breakfast?"

"It's even better when my husband makes it for me. So, thank you for making me breakfast." She smiled.

"Well, what can I say? I aim to please."

After eating, they each went their separate ways. "Have fun with Richard!" Phillip said as he walked out the door.

"Fun for who?"

Chapter 2

As Richard strolled into the precinct, he was welcomed by a detective leaving.

"Richard!"

"Jacob."

"Did you get your sugar this morning?"

"The only reason I'm in today," Richard said as he tapped him on the shoulder and kept walking to his desk. It was covered with case files that he was trying to close. Even the best detectives had to wait weeks for DNA results. Alice leaned on his stack of files, waiting.

"You better not be digging through my stuff. It's illegal to go through people's personal stuff."

Alice rolled her eyes. "Your filing system should be illegal. Look at this mess!"

Faking hurt, Richard rebutted, "Please, my filing system is spectacular. I file from most entertaining to least.

Every murder is a puzzle, and some puzzles are more challenging than others. After 13 years, my job is much more than saving lives. It's about being the best puzzle master ever."

Alice sighed. "The DNA results came back from one of our cases, and I'm trying to find the file. It's the piano wire case. Also, I've hear that spiel about a thousand time."

"Oh! The husband who killed his wife four months ago, because she was going to leave him when she found him cheating on her. He used the piano wires to make it seem that the piano teacher killed her. The husband's only alibi is the woman he was sleeping with. The file should be the fourth one at the bottom of the pile because it was slightly intriguing but still too easy. I did like the piano wires. Very original but he forgot that piano wires will cut you if you're not wearing gloves, which genius didn't wear."

"Found it! Were you saying something? Because we have a killer to go arrest."

"What's the hurry? It's not like he's going to kill anyone else."

"That is not the point!"

Annoyed Richard responded, "I already solved it. Can't we send someone else to go arrest him?"

"This is our case; we need to finish it ourselves. That's not how it works." She threw the paperwork at him as she made her way out the office.

They both got in her car and headed to Mr.Conley's last known location.

Alice shifted into gear. "So, I waited for you this morning."

"I wasn't feeling well this morning."

"You seem fine."

"Okay, I'm not going to lie to you, but Marc didn't want me to leave his side this morning. I tried my best, but I just couldn't say no to those eyes of his."

"Is that so?" Alice smiled.

"Yep, curse of being this handsome."

Alice let that sink in before exhaling from exhaustion. "So, how's everything been going with Marc?"

"Listen to this. He doesn't want me to go near his job, because it would look bad if it comes out that he's dating a cop."

"Doesn't that make it more interesting? We all know how you like interesting things."

"Maybe for him. I wouldn't care less."

"Sure, you wouldn't."

"What I really don't understand is how you ended with an English professor for a husband." Richard switched the subject.

"Helping people is my job. I've always been strong, so I never shy away from danger."

"Really? I thought only teddy bears got black belts?" Richard said snidely.

Alice exhaled. "Like I was saying, I don't know if I could do it if I was weak. My husband is a great guy. Strength is not what he's known for, but he never lets that prevent him from doing the right thing."

"Must be tiresome."

"I love it."

"Yeah, that sounds like true love to me," Richard answered looking in the distance.

"What about a detective dating a journalist? You could say it's meant to be." Alice smiled as she changed the subject back.

"Why did I let you meet him?"

"Like you had a choice. Anyway, here we are. This is his office."

"Let's do this."

Once they reached the building, the security guard asked them if they were here to see anyone. Alice flashed her badge. "Yes. We have a late appointment with Mr.Conley from E.B.C enterprise."

"E.B.C enterprise is on the 8th, 9th, and 10th floor. I don't know which floor he works on."

"Don't worry. We already know where his desk is," Richard said with a smile on his face.

"You seem to be enjoying yourself for someone that didn't even want to come along." Alice said to Richard as they stepped away.

"I have no idea what you're talking about."

"Sure."

They both walked past the security guard and caught his reflection speeding to the reception desk where he picked up the phone to make a call.

"Should we stop him?" Richard inquired.

"No. If Conley starts running then I can give him my regards from his dead wife."

"Do you remember what his car looks like?"

Alice glanced at him, "Do you know who you're talking to?"

Richard walked in the elevator while Alice walked straight ahead to the emergency staircase.

"Now, which floor was he on again? Oh, yeah, 8th floor."

As Richard made his way out of the elevator, he saw Mr. Conley speed-walking toward the emergency exit. Mr. Conley turned his head and saw Richard smirking at him. As Richard walked forward, he saw a jar of lollipops and slowed down, taking a lollipop from the reception desk. He yelled to Mr. Conley from across the room.

"We know you left the evidence at your house, and we will be taking you there once we arrest you."

Hearing that stopped Mr. Conley in his tracks. In a split second, he thought if he could escape and destroy any evidence, he could get away with his crimes. Mr. Conley bolted, running toward the emergency exit and flying down the stairs. Richard strolled towards the emergency exit and looked down the stairs to see Mr. Conley already on the 5th floor.

"Wow! Look at him go; how ever will I catch up to him?" Richard said sarcastically as he enjoyed his lollipop. Richard walked back toward the elevator.

Mr.Conley kept running. His mind raced with multiple thoughts: what his life would be like in jail. His heart was beating like never before. He felt that he was going to pass out but kept going because he knew he had to get out of there.

When he finally made it to the garage. He made a mad run towards his car, his heart beating faster as he got closer. When he could finally see it, a smile started to appear on his face. He could do this. He deserved a second chance, and his second chance was about to happen.

"You should have done more cardio. For a second I almost left." Alice said as she walked out from behind Mr. Conley's car.

He understood that she had a gun, but, if he got caught, it would be over for him. He decided to take a risk and push her out of the way—but as he got closer, he noticed that she didn't go for her gun. He got close enough that his fingers could touch Alice, and the next thing he felt was a sharp pain to his heart. He froze, and everything went dark.

"Goddammit, why did you knock him out? Now we have to carry him to the car." Richard said as he walked toward Alice.

"Honestly, I thought he was going be better than this."

"Well, you're a black belt. What did you expect?"

"Just bring the car here, and we'll just shove him inside. Problem solved."

Richard threw his cuffs at Alice as he caught her car keys in the air and reluctantly went to get the car.

Richard sat at his desk.

"Well, that's one boring case done and over with. I wish it was out of my expectation, you know?"

"At least we got a workout."

"Hey, I didn't want a workout. Which is why I took the elevator down like a civilized person."

"You complain the most for someone who doesn't put in any leg work."

"Excuse me! I told you that he was guilty four months ago, but noooo. You had to follow procedures." Richard joked.

"Too bad we can't arrest people just on your say so. Anyway, let's go get some coffee."

"Finally, you're speaking my language."

They both went to the coffee shop and returned to the precinct. That's when the call came from an officer on site.

Chapter 3

The night before....

In a small building far from the precinct, a small marketing agency was working late. They were finally able to get the big contract that was going to push them to the next level. They could finally grow from a team of 24 to one of over 50, which would allow them to take in even more contracts.

"This is it, team! We have worked so hard and so many late hours to be the best and get noticed by the big shots—and finally, we have gotten our chance. I'm proud of everyone here and I can't wait for us to become the top marketing firm in this country. For now, let's just cover all our bases, make sure there are no mistakes. Last stretch!" cheered Larry, along with his twelve employees.

"Does that mean we'll be able to hire additional people to work the late shift?" Sylvia joked.

"Why would I do that? I thought you liked working late."

"I'm such a professional, I make it look like I enjoy working late. Just remember that when you're giving the raises. Now, Mike here..." Sylvia turned to Mike, who was polishing off his third cup of coffee.

"Whoa! I fell asleep that one time!"

"I gave you all a great speech and this is the response I get. Anyway, let's bring this home." Larry turned to his computer.

Twenty minutes later, the internet went down.

"Shit, why now?! My system is down. How's yours?"

"It's not the system. It's the WiFi. I think we lost it."

"Are you kidding me?! Out of all times. Now?!"

"Let's see if we can get to the router and reset it. Does anyone know where the router is located?"

Everyone looked at each other with quizzical expressions.

William jumped up. "The cleaning lady! We can ask her. She might know where it's located."

"Good idea. Let's go look for her on a lower floor since she has yet to come to this one" Mike got up and made his way to the door.

William joined him by the elevator. They waited, but the elevator never arrived. Mike kicked the elevator door. "Shit! This stupid building always has an issue. Once we finish this deal, the boss better move us to a better building."

"So, stairs it is," William replied.

They both went down to the second floor.

"Anybody here?" William called out. They looked in every room with no luck.

"That's weird. I thought she was going to be here since all the lights are on."

"Maybe she came to this floor and went back down. Let's go to the lobby."

They made their way down the stairs to the lobby, where they finally saw the custodian. Excitedly, they ran towards her. At the sight of two men running toward her, she reluctantly stepped back a bit.

"So sorry, we didn't mean to scare you!" Mike smiled.

Averting her gaze, she answered, "I'm not scared."

"We just wanted to ask you a question." William said reassuringly.

Mike got straight to the point. "Yeah sorry about that, but would you happen to know where the router for the building is located?"

"The router?" She responded.

"Yes! The router! It's for the internet."

She gained back her courage to look them in the eye. "I'm sorry. I don't know. I just clean the offices."

"Damn! Okay. Let's think. It wasn't on the second floor, and I know it's not on the third floor, so let's check this floor," William responded.

The two of them started looking around for the router and couldn't find anything.

"She's very pretty, especially those eyes of hers," Mike whispered.

"We don't have time for this. I'm tired and want to go home. So, do me a favor and keep searching instead of getting distracted."

The door to the stairs opened. "Hey, what's taking so long!?" Sylvia poked her head out.

"We are having trouble finding the router. Even the custodian doesn't know where it is," William responded.

"It's probably in the basement, you morons." Sylvia rolled her eyes.

"Oh yeah, almost forgot about the basement," Mike responded.

The three of them left the cleaning lady and headed toward the basement door. They jiggled the doorknob but nothing happened.

"Great! First the elevator and now this. Could this night get any better?" Mike grumbled.

"Why not ask the cleaning lady if she has the keys?" Sylvia answered.

Mike and William set out again to find the custodian.

"Sorry for bothering you again, but would you happen to have the keys to the basement?" William asked.

"Yes, but I'm not supposed to let anyone in the basement," she shyly responded.

"I'm very sorry for asking but we have an emergency. The internet is down and we have a deadline to meet. So would you please let us in?" Mike said reassuringly.

She looked at them and could see the sincerity in their eyes. "Ok, but I have to come with you."

"Oh! Definitely you're doing us a favor. Thank you so much!"

She unlocked the door to the basement, and they all went down. They turned on the single light bulb which shone dimly through the room. They started looking around.

"I found it!" William yelled.

"Okay, let's reset it and get back to work, cause I'm ready to go home."

"It's not on to begin with. That could be the problem." William said as he pressed the on button.

It did not turn on.

Puzzled, he followed the power cord and realized that it was cut—and there was a paper wrapped around it.

This is a hunt. Screaming isn't going to do anything. No one will come because death is right behind you. The only way out is through blood. Let's begin.
We are EVO the Next Stage.

He turned toward the cleaning lady.

"Are you kidding me?! You think this is funny? We have work to finish, and you cut the wires?" Mike yelled.

"I..I.. didn't ...do this." she stammered with her lip quivering from fear.

"I don't think she's lying. Why would she cut the wire? Isn't it convenient that we also lost reception on our phones at the same time?" William stated.

They tried calling 911, but the call didn't go through.

"What does this mean?" Sylvia began to get alarmed.

"It means that we need to find the others." William turned to the cleaning lady. "And you should come with us."

They went upstairs to the lobby and tried to open the door to leave the building, but it was chained on the other side.

"Dammit!" Mike yelled.

"Stop shouting! You're making too much noise," William muttered.

"Oh! I'm sorry, I'm pissed that someone is trying to freaking kill us!"

"Yeah, and you're telling them where we are. Whoever wrote that note said it is a hunt. If this is not a game, we better start thinking of ourselves as the predators, not the prey. What would you do if you were a predator?"

"I don't care!" Mike exclaimed. "Okay, I just want to freaking go home! I don't freaking know what a killer would—"

William pushed him against the wall. Sylvia grabbed William, screaming, "What are you doing?!"

"I will not die today because of you. So, you better stop whining and start fighting. Let's regroup with the others," William growled at Mike.

"Don't be too hard on him." A voice came from behind them.

They turned to see a man in a white shirt, sleeves rolled up. His eyes violet. He spun a military knife in his left hand as he walked toward them. About ten feet away from them, he juggled the knife from his left hand to his right, grabbing it and pointing it at them.

"I see you like to push people. Not really my cup of tea. I prefer to just dislocate every bone in them while they're alive. Time consuming, but, hey, we all have our quirks. Anyway, the three of you can leave, but he's mine." The man pointed his knife at William.

"Don't listen to him! He's only one man! It's four of us. We can easily take him down!" Mike exclaimed.

The violet eyed man sighed with boredom. "I really don't want to kill the four of you, so I'll give you 10 seconds to decide. 10...9...8...7..."

William interrupted.

"The three of you leave and rejoin the others. Grab anything that can be used as a weapon and come back ready to fight. I'll hold him off." William cracked his knuckles.

They all looked at each other.

"I said, go!" William shouted.

Sylvia grabbed the cleaning lady's hand and ran past the killer, leaving her two co-workers behind. They ran up the stairs as she yelled. "I'm sorry!"

Holding his ground, Mike said, "I think two versus one is better."

"You sure about this?" William asked.

"Don't ask."

They turned to face the man.

"Hope you won't mind two versus one, since you have a knife and all."

"One or twenty; it doesn't make a difference. I just need one or two to be satisfied. And this knife is for you to use. It wouldn't be fun if it was too easy."

He placed the knife on the floor and kicked it their way.

Meanwhile, the two women continued up the stairwell without looking back. Sylvia pulled the cleaning lady, urging her to keep up, and desperately tried to wipe the tears that were blurring her vision. On the way to the third floor, she slammed into a bloody Larry.

"Run! There's two of them. Two crazy guys killing everyone upstairs!" Larry grabbed Sylvia.

Sylvia gasped. "No no no! What's going on? This can't be happening."

"There's one downstairs, also," the cleaning lady whispered.

Larry stopped in his tracks. "What do you mean there's one downstairs?"

"The front entrance was locked, then a guy came with a knife and told us he was going to kill us!" Sylvia explained.

"If you saw what they did upstairs, you would know that down is the only way. They were toying with us; they broke Benny in half—" He proceeded to throw up on the floor. "We're going to die."

"We can make it if we work together," Sylvia said unconvincingly.

As she finished her sentence, an object rolled from the third floor. Sylvia saw that it was Benny's head, with a piece of his spine stuck to it. She could tell that the head had been ripped off from the body. She had never seen anything like this. The cleaning lady beat her to it, screaming from the top of her lungs with Sylvia joining her.

"Sorry for interrupting. You were saying something about teamwork." A man covered in blood peered down at them, chuckling.

They looked up into his bright grey eyes.

"How many times do I have to tell you not to interrupt people when they're are talking?" A brown skin man appeared next to him.

The group couldn't see the stranger's eyes because his curly hair covered them. He passed his hands through his hair, slicking it back from his field of view, exposing his bright hazel eyes. That's when a cold chill ran down Sylvia's spine. It was like two monsters were staring down at them and all they could see was their crystal clear eyes; she'd never seen eyes so hazel or so gray.

She grabbed the cleaning lady by the hand and tried to drag Larry down the stairs, too, but his weight was too much for her. Larry had already given up; he let go of her hand and stayed behind for the inevitable.

The ladies reached the second floor, an open area full of desks and looked for a place to hide. Sylvia finally found a closet near the restroom that required a key.

"Do you have the key?!" Sylvia asked frantically.

The cleaning lady with trembling hands pulled out a big pile of keys. She fumbled through, unable to find the correct one.

"It's ok. It's going to be alright. Just breathe, and it will be fine." Sylvia kept peering at stairwell door, tears running down her cheeks, waiting for those monsters to appear.

The custodian took a deep breath and started looking for the key again. She finally found it and unlocked the door as both of them ran in and closed the door behind them. The closet was small and dark. Sylvia clenched the doorknob for what seemed to be like hours. After finally calming down, she realized her leg was warm and wet. She hadn't realized that she peed herself when she saw those two monsters staring down at her.

"I should have taken a survival class or a martial arts class," Sylvia whispered with a small chuckle.

The cleaning lady, still behind her, responded, "I think you're strong already. I'm still breathing because of you."

"When I was younger, there was a girl in my school that would always bully everyone because she came from money. Nobody did anything until the day my parents got arrested, and I wasn't strong anymore. Every time I look back, I feel ashamed for making life harder for my classmates and promised myself to never be that person again."

"You're not that person anymore."

"I never asked you, what's your name? I'm Sylvia by the way"

"You can call me Myra," the cleaning lady said as she snickered.

"What's so funny?"

"I was thinking about that old game Operation. The game where you have to get the pieces out right or it would buzz. In reality, people don't buzz. They normally scream."

The electrifying fear ran again through Sylvia's spine. She remembered that all three killers had bright colored eyes. She then realized there was one more person with such bright eyes: Myra.

She turned to the newly discovered monster. "What are you going to do to me?"

"Have you ever taken a second to smell some roses?"

Sylvia began to cry.

The monster stood up and peered at Sylvia. "Well, I have and honestly I don't get it at all. Roses smell like nothing to me. On the other hand, blood definitely does it for my brothers and me. Now, you Lessers smell like shit to us. There's nothing more that we want than to replace the smell of a Lesser with that of their blood. My two brothers upstairs like to rip their victims apart to get the blood all over their bodies. Now, my brother downstairs prefers to dislocate people's shoulders and legs. Once he's done, he'll cut your wrist, lie next to the body and start reading while you're slowly dying. As for me, you are about to find out."

Chapter 4

Richard and Alice pulled up to a squat gray office building surrounded by media and yellow crime scene tape.

"Look at them trying to make their way in," Alice said, annoyed.

"And look at this officer getting sick in front of the camera. Great way to tell them there's nothing going on."

"The cleanup crew is going to have a lot on their plate dealing with the journalists, but even with all that, I would rather be in their shoes right now," Alice grumbled.

"What!?! This is what I have been waiting for," Richard said with a smile." Let's go catch some real bad guys!"

"Yeah, I keep forgetting how weird you are," she said, rolling her eyes at Richard as she got out of her car.

They pushed their way into the building and were immediately bombarded with the smell of death. Laying before them on the marble floor were two dead bodies.

"Dead bodies right at the entrance; a great way of saying hello," Richard said sarcastically.

Alice ignored Richard and started to analyze the scene. "So, we have two dead bodies lying on top of each other. Their bones seem to have been dislocated."

An officer walked up to the detectives. "We're guessing it's a team of killers, one holding the weapon and maybe the others dislocating what seems to be every bone in the victims' bodies."

Alice cut in, "This was done by one person."

"Why do you think so?" the police officer asked.

"This entrance is too narrow. It would be hard to have more than four people in it and control the situation." Alice responded as she crouched down to stare at the bodies.

Richard followed, "Did you notice no gun wound?"

"Yeah, so we have someone who is very confident in their strength to beat two guys and dislocate all their bones."

"How can you tell they didn't use a gun to scare them?" the officer jumped in.

Richard sighed with annoyance. "Let's say you're seeing someone getting their bones dislocated, hearing their screams. Would they be able to stay still? Most likely they would try to fight back or run which would result in them getting shot. Staying still when someone points a gun at you is easy; staying still when you're watching someone get tortured is hard."

Alice pointed to the victim's hand. " Or you can just look at the knuckles, there's some skin abrasions. They fought back."

Richard looked at Alice. "You're no fun, but seriously how good is this guy?"

"Very. He didn't just go straight for the kill which would have been easier. From the moment he started, he knew there was no way he could lose. That is not just confidence. That is a whole lot of experience. Most likely he took their knee out first to control the situation after toying with them."

Richard turned to the officer. "Where are the crime scene investigators? The medical examiner? Anyone with forensic competence?"

"Well, these two bodies are only the beginning. The ME has her hands a little full." He turned away. "I'll get an investigator down here to fill you in."

"That's one way to get rid of him. So, what do you think?" Alice questioned Richard.

"Look at the bodies. They're mangled together into a crescent moon. And look at the blood. It's like it's following a stream."

"We know that he had a knife to cut the femoral arteries." Alice bent down to look at the dried blood on the floor to see a small crevice in it. "He used a knife to create a line on the floor so the blood would go where he wants."

"It looks like a box. He used the bodies and blood to create his own little box."

"Great, we are looking for a guy who's 6 feet and looking for a safe space." Alice replied sarcastically.

"Hope I'm not interrupting." The crime scene investigator joined Alice and Richard.

"No, you're not. So, what can you tell us about what happened here?"

"We have fourteen victims. We have these two here with the cut arteries and dislocated bones. On the second floor, we have two more victims. And on the third floor, we have a severed head and a body. Lastly, on the fourth floor we have the remaining victims." The investigator took a break and collected himself. "I've truly never seen anything like this."

"Fantastic! Let's go check out the rest of this crime scene," Richard said with a smile, as he walked past the investigator.

"Sorry about him. You know how he can be," Alice said.

"I need to step out for a minute, but we have Yasmin upstairs. She'll tell you what you need to know."

"Are you okay, Frank?"

"I'm not... I'm really not."

"I'm sorry."

"Just go. I'll be fine."

Alice and Richard walked to the second-floor corridor where they spotted two officers standing outside a restroom.

"I know where we need to go."

"You don't say."

As they walked through the door, they were welcomed by Yasmin taking photos. In front of them, two naked bodies hung from the ceiling by their hands. Two cuts continuous ran down their bodies, beginning from the inside of each of their arms, down their torsos all the way to their ankles. Under each of them sat a glass cube into which their blood drained. Floating on top of the vases of blood were blood-soaked white rose petals.

"Wow!" Richard gasped.

Alice exhaled. "Okay, this is next level."

Yasmin joined in, "You're telling me."

Richard jumped straight to the point. "What can you tell us?"

"Obviously, they were hung to the celling and one cut was done from their arms all the way down to their ankles. The cuts are deep but also smooth almost like a scalpel was use or something as sharp. Finally, draining all the blood into each glass container filled with fresh white rose pedals. Alive."

"I would also assume they were probably paralyzed." Alice interjected looking at the walls around them.

"Makes sense. You wouldn't stay still if you were hanging and being cut. Plus, there would be more blood on the wall than what I am seeing."

Alice walked up closer to the two bodies. "Those hooks on the ceiling that the bodies are hanging on, are they new?"

"I believe the killer put the hooks there and put this glass box afterward." She pointed to the cube on the floor.

"So, we are dealing with a killer that's very handy."

"They drilled a hole in the ceiling and there is no debris on this floor."

"I would assume any dust would be under the pool of blood under them," Yasmin replied.

Richard bent down to get a closer look at the pool of blood. "I don't think so. The whole point of this glass box is to admire the blood. Otherwise, they could have easily let the blood drain to the floor. Plus putting the pedal of roses in there shows that this is some sort of art to them. Most likely they cleaned the floor after they set up everything. So, the question is: did they take the trash and clothes with them or put it in a garbage can somewhere in the building?"

Alice turned to one of the officers in the room, "Could you have an officer check the garbage cans inside and outside the building?"

Alice turned to Yasmin. "How long will it take for us to get the report on our desk?"

"Normally this would take about three weeks, but since this case is going to be high profile, I'll get it on your desk within a week."

"Great, because the Captain is going to come down on us to get this resolved as quickly as possible." Alice turned to Richard. "Are you ready for the next body?"

"Absolutely."

"I'm going to finish here, and I'll join you in a bit. Just don't touch anything or move anything!"

As they walked away, Alice turned to Richard. "Different way of killing. Most likely different killers."

Richard responded confidently, "I would also bet you that the killer upstairs is different. It's like every killer had their own floor."

"The murders are very different from each other, so they're not worried about us knowing there's a group of them."

"There was no hesitation in the kills; each cut was smooth, so this is not their first rodeo—besides, this is too big a scale for first timers. Which mean that they've been killing outside our jurisdiction or under our nose."

"There's also a high level of trust between them. They walked in confident that each of them would fulfill their part, controlling fourteen people, without one of them escaping, and not leaving anyone alive for us to question."

"Well, let's go check the third floor."

As they walked upstairs, they saw another group of officers. A mutilated body and a severed head lay on the floor next to the bloodstained wall.

Richard looked up. "I'm guessing the rest of him is upstairs."

"A different style of killing," Alice said, ignoring him. They both looked closer at the body.

"Can't tell what's worse, the vomit or the blood." Richard exhaled. "This one is very gruesome compared to the others. I can see the other two people working together, but this one, I find harder to believe."

"For something like this, you wouldn't bring someone that can't control themselves. This is probably part of the ritual," Alice said as she looked at the bodies.

"I guess the other question is: why did he get killed here in the staircase? Was the culprit running after him? If that was the case, he wouldn't have stopped."

"Maybe one of the killers downstairs caught him on their way up."

"No, let's think about it for a second. Every one of the murders that we've seen so far took time. So that would mean one of them left their post. Considering how detail-oriented they are, that's very unlikely."

"They must have been here for a while, setting up. I would assume they were each waiting on their designated floor before starting."

"They locked the entrance door and hid until they were ready."

"We still only have half the picture. Let's get upstairs."

They finally arrived on the last floor to see a massacre. Bodies were ripped apart and there was blood everywhere.

Alice gasped. "This is insane."

Richard stared in amazement. "I have to agree."

"To have more than one suspect with the same level of cruelty."

"This room is too big for just one person to manage it."

"So how many murderers did we have on this floor?"

"It's rare to have multiple killers with the same style but two people wouldn't be enough to control everyone in this room."

"Well, if it was two of the same killers as downstairs then yes, they could." Alice responded.

"What type of monsters are we dealing with?" Richard smiled.

Chapter 5

Alice drove home after what seemed like an endless night. Once she parked her car, she sat there for a couple of minutes, closing her eyes to compose herself, then stepped out with the file in her hand. She walked inside.

"Welcome home, my love!" Phillip said, embracing her and kissing her softly.

"I love it when you welcome me home like this," she responded.

"Why do you think I do it?" he remarked with a flirtatious smirk.

"It's like you have an ulterior motive."

"What? Me? Never!"

"Did you forget? I'm a detective," she whispered in his hears.

"Oops! Looks like I got figured out."

"Something smells nice," Alice said, as she turned her head toward the table.

"Well! I couldn't let you go hungry after a long day," he responded with a smile.

"Can't wait."

Alice went to her home office, put the file on her desk, and went back to the dining room to have dinner with Phillip.

"How was work?" Alice asked Phillip while they were eating.

"Remember how I told my students what to study for their exams?"

"Let me guess, they didn't study," she responded with a smirk.

"Not only did they not study, but some of them didn't even bother answering the extra credit questions."

"You're nicer than me. If I were in your shoes, they wouldn't even be getting extra credit."

"I figure they have a lot on their plates and wanted to help them a bit."

"They're in college! It's supposed to be hard."

"It shouldn't be that hard. Having to work and go to school full time, paying rent while accumulating debt that they can't repay. I don't envy them."

"Sounds like you should go into politics," she responded with a smile. She loved how caring Phillip could be.

"Great news! I don't need to. Neveah Orcus just announced she's running for Mayor. She has amazing policies and she's a Nova. Our city could be one of the first to have a Nova in leadership. She left her home! Do you know how rare it is for Novas to leave their home? Just her being out put her life in danger. She's so amazing."

"Honey, I love your optimism, but you shouldn't trust people that go into politics too much."

"She's different! I can feel it. Plus, it's not like she's a real politician."

"True, but she just started. So, instead of believing in her from the start, watch what she does then decide if she's worth believing in."

"You're no fun." He pouted. "On a more positive note, I just heard back from HR. When we decide to have kids, they would get full scholarships."

"Well, that's a lot of money we would save!" She smiled.

"So, whenever you're ready to have kids, I'm here for you."

"Oh, are you?" Alice said sarcastically. "Soon, my love." She grabbed his hands and put a smile on his face.

"How bad was it today?" He asked her while drying the plates after their dinner.

She stopped washing the dishes for a second and kept looking down. After a long pause, she answered, "A massacre. That's what I would say."

"You've never used that word before."

"I've also never seen what I saw today."

"Whatever it is, nobody can handle it better than you and Richard," Phillip cheered her on only to have a plate slip out of his hands but caught by Alice and handed back to him.

"On the plus side, we closed one of our cases today," she said as she kept washing the dishes.

"Evil beware of my beautiful wife," he chanted while she laughed.

At the end of the night, Phillip went to bed, and Alice stayed up late to work on the case. She went into her home office and poured herself a scotch neat. This was not her normal routine, but cases like this one warranted a drink. She opened the file in front of her and took a sip.

"Show me what you got."

Chapter 6

Two days later, in one of the top investment firms in the country, Jeff speed walked past his co-workers, finally stopping in front of Maxwell's office.

"Okay, you're going to have to tell me your secret!" Jeff asked as he stepped in.

"Which secret are you interested in? Being an amazing husband or getting richer?" Maxwell responded as he got up from behind his mahogany desk.

"Definitely the getting richer part! Did you hear about the marketing firm massacre?"

Maxwell went to his bar cart and poured himself a drink. "Of course. It's my job to know about everything that happens."

"Well, thanks to you, we made millions. Can you believe we almost invested in them?"
He sniffed his whiskey and took a sip. "I just didn't see a need to invest in them. Yes, they had potential, but when I

met their CEO, I knew he didn't have what it took. I can't even remember his name, to be honest with you."

"That's a little harsh."

"We are in the business of making money. Harsh is just another avenue of that."

"What about telling us to invest in the security companies?"

Maxwell walked up to him and stared him down. "There's no such thing as lasting peace in this world."

Upon hearing that, a shiver ran down Jeff's spine, and he started to sweat. He then felt a pat on his shoulder.

"Just kidding, I just lucked out. It could have easily gone the opposite way," Maxwell said reassuringly.

"Sure. Anyone else I would believe, but you, not so much."

"Are you saying I don't have a believable face? Because that would be a problem for me."

"Not when you're smirking like that. Anyway, we are going to have a party later for this sudden burst of luck. Since you will be getting a hell of a bonus for this, I'm expecting you to come and pay for our drinks. It's only fair."

"I really wish I could, but the missus and I have something planned for today. Sorry."

"It's always about the missus with you. Well, next time, then." Jeff said as he walked out of Maxwell's office.

"Next time, definitely."

Maxwell informed his secretary not to disturb him for the next half hour. He then went back to his seat and loosened his tie, letting out a deep breath. He pulled out the necklace that he had hidden under his t-shirt, opened the small vial that was attached to it, and took a whiff.

"Finally," Maxwell whispered. "This is why I need to take a week off after cleansing. I need to slowly get used to the foul odor." He took a couple more whiffs and got up. "Well, I guess I can get there early."

He hid the vial of blood back in his shirt and fixed his tie. He called his secretary into his office. "I have an emergency that just came up and will have to leave early today."

"It's everything ok?" she inquired.

"Yes, it's just a family emergency. Jeff can take over during the upcoming meeting. Would you mind informing him of the change? I sent you all the information he will need. All he needs to do is show up."

"I will take care of that. Anything else?"

"That should be everything, but if something comes up, just give me a call. Keep an eye out during the meeting to see how Jeff handles it."

"I understand. Should I reschedule your meetings tomorrow?"

"I should be back tomorrow. If anything happens, I'll keep you posted," he answered as he put on his blazer and walked past his secretary.

He got into his car and turned off his GPS and his phone. He drove for about an hour, checking frequently to make sure that he was not being followed. His journey led him to an abandoned factory with broken windows and graffiti on the walls. There was a homeless man lying on the floor near the entrance. As soon as the homeless man saw Maxwell, he got up and rushed toward him. The man stopped in his tracks when he saw Maxwell's violet eyes. He could tell that getting any closer would get him killed.

"Forgive me, my God, for sullying your presence with the stench of my flesh." The homeless man quivered. He pulled out a hidden knife and slit his hand. As his blood dripped on the ground, he walked toward the door of the factory and opened it for Maxwell.

"Are my brothers and sister here yet?" Maxwell asked after entering.

"The other gods haven't arrived yet," the homeless man answered while staring at the floor.

Maxwell turned toward him. "Go wrap your wound and have another follower replace you for my sister and brothers' welcoming."

"Yes, my God," he responded as he left.

The inside of the factory was filthy. There was broken glass on the floor and some furniture scattered here and there. There were 2 elevators in the back of the building. It was dark even though it was still sunny outside. It was not a place anyone else would want to be at night.

Maxwell made his way to the elevator. When the door opened there was graffiti inside.

"Welcome my gods"

He got in and pressed the button for the basement. The basement was different from upstairs. It looked like it had just been renovated, everything was clean and modern. As he stepped off the elevator, he was welcomed by another follower.

"My God, thank you for blessing us with your presence, but your lowly servant wasn't prepared for such an early visit and hasn't readied the sacrifice yet."

"It's all right; the sacrifice will proceed when my brothers and sister arrive."

"Thank you, my God! In the meantime, is th-," before he could finish, a woman arrived.

"My God, I have prepared your room for you," she said, cutting into the conversation confidently.

Maxwell headed down the corridor and into his private room. His siblings had their own private rooms, too, but they didn't spend as much time in their rooms as Maxwell did. Maxwell was the only one who always arrived an hour early for their meetings. He pulled out a book from his bookshelf.

"This is new," he said to himself.

"I figured you would want to read something that's new, my God," the woman from before said, standing in the doorway behind him.

"Elaine, what are you doing here?"

"I knew there was a meeting, so where else would I be but your side," she responded with a smile, looking directly into his violet eyes.

"The meeting is in a couple of hours. Shouldn't you be at home instead?" he asked calmly as he sat down and opened the book.

She walked to the bed and bent down to plug in a scent diffuser into the outlet and walked back to Maxwell. "I am your personal servant. Of course, I would be where you need me, my God."

"I take it that my concierge called you," he responded while continuing to read.

"But of course. It's a wife's duty to know where her husband is at all times and a servant's duty to be available for their Gods at all times," she answered with a smile.

Maxwell stopped reading and looked at Elaine. "It smells nice in here."

"I figured it would please you. It's a plug-in fragrance that mimics the smell of blood. Made it myself."

Maxwell smiled at Elaine "Thanks". He got up from his chair and walked toward the door to lock it. He turned to face Elaine "We have a couple of hours before the others arrive."

"I guess it is time for my blessing." She smirked as she removed her dress.

Two hours had passed before there was a knock on Maxwell's door.

"My God, the Goddess is requesting your attendance before the meeting."

"Inform her that I will join her soon!" he yelled as he came out the shower.

"Yes, my God."

Maxwell put his clothes on to go see his sister.

"Will you be all right?" Elaine inquired while laying naked in bed.

"I think it's more dangerous if I were to stay in the room with you," he flirted as he got closer to Elaine and gave her a long, deep passionate kiss, leaving her wanting more.

"Would that be a problem?"

"Don't worry. We'll be alone again when we get home, he said as he left the room.

Lately, he had been nervous to see his sister. He could read his two brothers. They were simple; they just wanted to kill—but his sister was different. He couldn't read her anymore. The only thing he used to be sure of was that they would never hurt each other, but ever since Maxwell married Elaine, he worried that his sister might have changed. She wasn't opposed to them getting married; her problem was how close they were. He finally arrived in front of his sister's room. He took a second to compose himself before going in.

"How long are you going to stand in front of the door?" a voice came from inside.

Maxwell exhaled and opened the door. There his sister was in the room. She seemed to be working on something while giving her back to him. "Heard you were looking for me," he said

The woman turned around and got up from her desk. "Well, of course, I was! I couldn't wait to see my brother." She was wearing a slim, reddish-black, 3-piece suit with red stilettos, which gave her the same height as Maxwell.

"You look better in this outfit than the cleaning lady's uniform," he laughed.
She walked toward her minibar and poured two glasses of whisky. "How rude! I look great in everything. I think it's a curse." She then handed Maxwell a glass.

Maxwell took a sip. "So, why am I really here, Myra?"

Myra walked back to her desk, pulled out a picture and showed it to Maxwell. Upon seeing the photo, he slammed his drink on the table and snatched it to have a closer look.

"What is this!?" he growled in disbelief while looking at a picture of a dead man.

"Isn't it obvious?"

"This is not funny!" he yelled while gripping at her blazer.

Myra, still composed, grabbed his hands and removed them from her.

"Enough, Brother," she responded in a serious tone which brought Maxwell back to his senses but deeper into sadness, because he realized what he was seeing. He tried to regain his composure, but he was still shaken by the picture. He closed his eyes. "How?"

"A broken neck."

"Who was it that killed our brother?"

"I don't know," she answered, frustrated.

"What do you mean, you don't know? You found us and made this whole cult but you can't find the murderer?"

Myra started laughing maniacally. "Oh, that was a good one. Murderer. Are you really one to say that word? If our brother was killed, it's because he was weak. We were bred to be killers, but he went and got himself kill instead. The better question is. Was he targeted? How would you answer that?" She asked Maxwell.

Maxwell took a deep breath and regained his calmness and thought about it for a second. "No average human could kill us, only a Nova could. So, yes."

"Correct. And now the even better question is: Was it for revenge or was it because he was an EVO?"

"So, we have a Nova out there whose hunting us," he said with a smile, realizing he would get to kill the person that killed his brother.

"Yeah, and he likes to show off. Breaking someone's neck means you have to get close and personal."

"Do you think our brother could have been slacking?"

"Who knows? We have been separated over fifteen years. Probably not. Look at Ethan and James. When's the last time they actually trained?"

"There's three Novas in the city. Do you think it's them?"

"Doubt it. Neveah is running for mayor and the other two are her bodyguards. They have too much attention on them right now to kill anyone."

"Wait! Does the police have his body?"

"No. Apparently the body disappeared before they could do an autopsy."

"Good job."

"That wasn't me," she replied.

"So, the killer?"

"Yeah." She took the picture from Maxwell and burned it in her fireplace. "James and Ethan cannot find out about this. They will leave to get vengeance for our brother."

"What makes you think I won't leave?"

"How's Elaine been doing lately?" she asked.

"So, why are you telling me?"

"Because if one of us has been killed, I want you to keep an eye out, because we are probably being watched." She unbuttoned her blazer and removed it, then proceeded to take off her shoes.

"Should we postpone the plan?" he asked.

She walked back to her desk. "Since we were released into this world, we haven't faced any challenges. Everything has always gone the way we planned. Now, for the first time, there might be a wrench. So, why should we postpone our plan? On the contrary, I'm looking forward to meeting them," she answered as she went back to what she was doing.

"I couldn't agree more," Maxwell said as he exited her room.

As the time for the meeting approached, he headed to the conference room. Upon opening the door, he was met with James's familiar bright hazel eyes and dark complexion. He walked toward Maxwell, and they greeted each other with a brotherly hug.

"Wow, I can't believe I'm seeing the great James all by himself," Maxwell said jokingly. "Where's Ethan?"

A voice came from behind. "Why? Want an autograph?" A man with gray colored eyes and pale skin responded, laughing as he entered into the room. His face and shirt were stained with blood.

"Ethan, you should have changed before coming," Maxwell responded.

"My bad." Ethan took his shirt off, revealing his sculpted body. He used his shirt to wipe the blood from his face and threw it on the floor.

"Don't throw it on the floor! Just have your Lesser take care of it."

"She's indisposed at the moment," James answered with a smile.

"You slept with her?! I thought you said you would never use the cream," Maxwell questioned James.

"And I didn't. I prefer the scent to be uninhibited. I prefer real blood," James replied.

"We just had a little fun, that's all," Ethan responded with a smile.

Myra walked in. "Let's begin."

They each took a seat.

"How was last night?" Myra asked.

"Being able to rip those Lessers to pieces and inhaling their sweet scents was just simply amazing."

"Seeing the different emotions on their faces was the best part. First, it was hope when I threw them the knife. Then despair when they realized that I was toying with them. Every hit released a small, beautiful fragrance. In the end I was able to read a nice book while being surrounded by it. How about you?" Maxwell turned to Myra.

"It's always funny seeing how the lambs act when they don't realize they're in the wolf's den. Being stuck in a small closet with your predator. It was better than I imagined. But something was lacking. We have everything that we could ever want. We are smarter than the average person, stronger than the average person. The one thing that we have never experienced is a real challenge. It would be nice if they did something out of our control for once."

"I guess that's one of the curses that we have to live with."

"Curses are meant to be broken," James answered as he high fived Ethan.

"True, so let's move to the next plan. Let's see what Alice and Richard can do to break our curse."

There was a knock on the door. "The sacrifice is ready for you, my gods."

As Elaine walked in, Ethan and James showed a sign of disgust by frowning. Myra exhaled. "Dear, it seems you forgot to put your cream on." As Myra was about to get off her chair, Maxwell jumped up and slapped the table "Get out now!" he yelled.

Elaine quickly apologized and left.

"Maxwell, you shouldn't be so harsh on your wife. Mistakes happen," Myra said with a smile.

"I think we should have James's Lesser start the sacrifice instead," Maxwell said, changing the subject.

"Not going to be possible. Ethan killed him." James answered with a laugh.

"What? So, we only have my and Ethan's personal Lessers left?"

"We were bored, so we had our Lessers fight each other to the brink of death. The winner got our personal blessing, and the loser got to see us smile one last time," Ethan grinned as he replied.

"Weren't your Lessers married to each other?"

"That made it even more fun: Seeing them go at it to spend the night with one of us."

Myra burst into hysterical laughter. "Oh, that is rich!" She wiped the tears out of her eyes. "This is what it means to be gods. Our wish is their wish. Our happiness is their happiness. Their devotion is only one-sided. If they couldn't kill each other at our will, then this cult that I created would be nothing but garbage," her tone quickly got sterner.

"If we are gods then what is Mother?" Maxwell asked as the room went silent. He could see annoyance on his siblings' faces.

Myra turns to Maxwell. "If we are Gods, then she can only be the Devil, and it's time to kill the Devil

Chapter 7

After the meeting they all went their separate ways. When Maxwell got home, Elaine apologized to him about her mistake and thanked him for saving her. Elaine of all people knew that if Maxwell had not kicked her out of the room, Myra would have killed her.

Maxwell also believed that it was partially his fault that she forgot to put the cream on after taking a bath. The cream was infused with blood and decreased the human scent that disgusted them so much. Maxwell got close to Elaine and held her in his arms. "Please don't let that happen again. I might not be there to intervene."

Hearing that made Elaine happy, because her God and husband cared for her. She knew that had Maxwell not been there, she would have been killed. In the past, she would have been happy dying for her gods, but now, she didn't want the moments she had with Maxwell to end-and he felt the same. He tried to hide how much she meant to him, not just because she was a Lesser, but also because he knew that if his sister or brothers found out, she would be in danger.

As Elaine fell asleep in their bed, Maxwell couldn't help but think of how he had fallen, that he was brought to his knee by her. It used to be just him, going out at night looking for Lessers to quench the urges. He targeted the homeless; dealing with them was easier for him, because the human stench was covered by the smell of homelessness. Sometimes he would go for a person that was well-known mostly because of the challenge, but it always turned out the same: boring. Until that night.

He decided to go to a company party, celebrating a great quarter, when he smelled the scent he knew too well: blood. He slowly followed the scent, which took him to Hayes. Maxwell thought of every possibility. Maybe he had cut himself, but something was telling him it was not so. Maxwell grew curious about him and started keeping an eye on him, and it wasn't long until his suspicion came true. He saw Hayes kill a homeless man, which piqued Maxwell's curiosity. Maxwell had a policy to never kill close to home, nor would he harm people that he had met at any point—but he was getting bored. He felt that he was just repeating the same actions every day without change.

He wanted his heart to beat. He wanted to remember the fear he had during his first kill. He decided that he was going to kill Hayes—not to stop him, but because he wanted to know how the blood of a killer smelled. He waited four months, patiently getting ready, while following Hayes. He had built a map of Hayes's life in his head. He was excited. This was fun for him like a little kid doing a bigger puzzle for the first time. Maxwell was ready to move. He knew where to go.

Work had been getting stressful for Hayes lately, which was Maxwell's doing. He was dropping fake investment hints, causing Hayes to keep losing money and struggling to make his quota without ever meeting him in person. Maxwell made sure to push Hayes to the limit; now he just waited for the breaking point. One night, Hayes went to an empty park, known to be a haven for the homeless. He waited patiently until he saw his target. As he started walking toward the sleeping homeless on the bench, Maxwell came out of the bushes, wrapped his arms around his neck, and pulled him into the bushes, maintaining the chokehold until he passed out. Maxwell carried the unconscious Hayes to his car. No one ever suspect the guy carrying the drunk person away. Maxwell drove to an abandoned building and woke Hayes up.

"Where the hell is this?!" Hayes asked as he got up.

"My playground," Maxwell replied.

"Maxwell? What's going on?! What did you do to me?!"

Maxwell rolled up his sleeves. "I know we haven't really met in person, and sorry for putting so much work on you, but have you finished the financial report? Cause I needed those yesterday."

"Is this a freaking prank? I don't know where I am, and you're asking about reports!" Hayes snapped.

"I get that you're angry, but think about it from my perspective: you won't live past tonight. So, figuring out if those reports are already done now will be easier than waiting the right amount of time to ask your boss without being insensitive," Maxwell said, using air quotes.

"What do you mean I won't live past today?"

"Do you also have to deal with so much disbelief when you kill people?"

"Wait! What?! I've never hurt anyone in my life!"

"Stop. You're making a fool out of yourself," Maxwell said without batting an eyelash.

Hayes started laughing, "So, when did you find out?"

"When you stole one of my prey, a couple of months ago."

"So, you, too."

"Please don't compare us. You're not even in my league."

Hayes snickered. "So, you're not just this arrogant at work, I see."

"That all depends on perspective. For example, I think you're the arrogant one thinking you're my equal when we both know that's not true."

"Funny coming from the man who wants to kill me because I poached on his turf."

"Oh, you think this is a turf battle? No. This is just curiosity. I want to know how your blood differs in smell."

"So, the smell of blood is your thing. For me it's power, knowing my life is worth more than everyone else's. The more I kill the more my value goes up."

"It's nice, isn't it, to have someone to talk to about all of this? But enough talking; let's start enjoying ourselves." Maxwell pointed to a knife that sat next to Hayes.

"Too bad you don't know who you're up against," Hayes said. He picked up the knife and checked the sharpness.

"Is that so?" Maxwell responded with a smile.

Hayes rushed toward Maxwell with a fury of slashes that only cut air. He started losing hope when he realized that Maxwell hadn't attacked him even once—and worst of all, he was smiling the whole time. That was Hayes's thing; he was supposed to be smiling over Maxwell's dead body. Maxwell finally got tired of watching Hayes's desperate failed attempt at killing him and decided to attack. He grabbed Hayes's wrist, causing him to drop the knife, and quickly followed with a punch to his side. The hit landed and lifted Hayes off his feet and onto the floor. Hayes coughed out blood as he tried to crawl away.

Maxwell could smell it in the air. "Very saturated. Interesting," Maxwell said.

Hayes, in a desperate attempt, kept throwing whatever he could find on the ground at Maxwell. He was like a wounded animal, and Maxwell was enjoying seeing him struggle like the Lesser he was. Hayes picked up a piece of glass on the floor and stood back up to face Maxwell.

"You couldn't do anything to me with a knife. What could you do with that?"

"I'll survive, I'll survive. I have value," Hayes kept mumbling as he attacked with the broken glass, but Maxwell reacted faster and punched him at full force on his temple. The second his fist hit Hayes, he heard a cracking sound and knew it was over. The man went flying toward a wall. As quickly as his happiness came, so had it ended. He smelled the blood on his fist, which relaxed him. "I need to do this again," he said out loud.

"Wasn't that fun?" a voice said from behind him. Maxwell reacted instantly by turning around with a right hook which was immediately blocked by the unknown person.

"Is that how you greet your long-lost sister?"

"Myra, is that you?'

"I was worried you were going to say Michelle."

"Please. How could I have mistaken you two?"

Myra helped Maxwell get rid of the body by burying it, and they reminisced for over an hour until he finally asked the question.

"So, why are you really here?"

"I've been looking for our sister and brothers?"

"Why?"

"To find Mother, of course."

"You mean the woman who threw us out after making us think we were special."

"But don't you want to know why?"

Of course, he wanted to know why they had been abandoned and why he was separated from the only family he could connect with. "You shouldn't have to ask. We were only 14 when she sent us to live with those fake parents. Only for them to disappear when I turned 21."

"So your fake parents disappeared."

"Didn't yours?"

"I killed them myself. I made sure to question them about Mother, but I couldn't get anything out of them."

"Too bad."

"It did get me thinking. Our existence must be a secret from the world, and for Mother to be able to keep that secret, she must have a massive amount of influence."

"That's if she was the one in control. For all we know, we might have been a by-product of this country's army to fight the Meneans, especially their Novas."

"It seems you don't think rationally when it comes to Mother," she said with a smirk. "I don't blame you."

"I guess I don't."

"It doesn't have anything to do with the military. If it did, then we would be a successful experiment. Look at us! We are walking killing machines, wouldn't you say? And if we were failures then we would have been killed instead of being let out. As for the Novas, I've never gone against one."

"True."

"I have been working on creating a cult."

Maxwell burst out laughing. "Let me guess: you want me to join."

She looked straight into Maxwell's eyes. "Yes," she answered.

"Why should I join a cult?"

"If we want to find Mother, then we have to do something big to get her attention. Anything we do will require people that are willing to die for us."

Maxwell thought about it. "I see. People that are willing to jump off a bridge if we ask them to."

"Exactly. I already found some people that are down in their luck and I used my strength and other skills to make them believe we are new gods."

"Gods? That's funny."

"If you find someone desperate enough to find meaning, and they believe you are the answer, they will follow you for life. Especially those Nova worshippers."

"What about the smell?"

Myra reached into her pocket and threw a small bottle at Maxwell "This is a special mixture of blood and cream. We just need to make sure they put it on before being in our presence."

Maxwell opened the bottle and took a whiff. "Not like the pure thing but not bad. It will do."

"So, do you want to find Mother?" she asked one more time.

Maxwell took a second to answer, "Count me in."

"Great. Now I just need to convince James and Ethan."

He couldn't hold his excitement and grabbed Myra. "Wait, you found them?" he asked.

"You don't know?"

"What?"

"You should read a magazine sometime. You might be surprised."

"What do you mean?" he asked hesitantly.

"They're models."

That was the beginning of the cult. Myra convinced James and Ethan to join. She purchased an abandon factory and used it as a base of operation. She was the leader of the facility and took care of the everyday work like recruiting and planning how best to bring Mother to them. Maxwell was there for support if she needed a hand. As for James and Ethan, they were the enforcers. They instilled fear in the Lessers to keep them in check and at the same time charmed them to do whatever they asked. Myra wanted to create a hierarchy among the Lessers, so she created roles. Personal Lessers served them directly and relayed their messages to the rest of the Lessers.

James and Ethan were the first two to get personal Lessers. Myra set up a selection process to pick her personal Lesser: they had to be able to last ten seconds against her. Many Lessers tried, but all of them were crush by Myra before the ten second were up. She did it with such amazing skill that the rest of the Lessers started believing even more that they were gods. In the end no Lesser was able to qualify. As for Maxwell, he never bothered looking for a Lesser.

As time passed, the cult had 40 Lessers that believed them to be gods. Myra created four additional roles within the cult. There were caretakers who took care of everyone in the cult and the facility, supporters whose job was to bring money to the cult, gatherers who were supposed to gather information on who they would kill, and chasers who hunted for sacrifice and defended the facility. Fitness was a must in the facility, especially for the chasers. They were required to spend more than four hours per day keeping their bodies in shape. The rest only had to spend an hour, but everyone needed to know how to fight.

Myra was in charge mostly of the gatherers and the chasers, while Maxwell was in charge of the supporters. Myra put Ethan and James in charge of the caretakers, mostly because the caretakers could function by themselves. Since Ethan and James didn't like to bother with what they deemed beneath them, it worked out perfectly. Maxwell's being in charge of the supporters meant that he had to take care of the finance of the facility and every member of the team. If the facility needed something, he would split it between the ten supporters to make it look less suspicious than one person buying eight treadmills.

There was one woman on the support team, Elaine, who stood out to Maxwell more than the rest. She was always there when he was. On some occasions Maxwell would see her working out in the gym facility as he left. Out of the ten supporters he was managing, Elaine was bringing in the most money, but she also clocked the most fitness hours. Maxwell decided to have a chat with her regarding her fitness hours since he found them to be excessive for a member of the support team. One evening, on his way out, he saw Elaine in the fitness room. He stopped and walked in. Seeing Maxwell, Elaine stopped what she was doing. "Sorry, my God, for letting you see me in this state," she said, out of breath.

"It's fine. You are doing what you are supposed to do."

She regained her breath and looked Maxwell in his bright violet eyes. She couldn't look away; she found it to be breathtaking. "Is there something that my God wants?"

"Actually, I was measuring the performance of the team and needed to talk to you about it."

"Is my performance inadequate?"

"No, you are actually excelling compared to the other members of the team, but I'm going to need you to decrease your fitness hours. It would be bad if you burn out."

She tilted her head down. "Forgive me, my God, I didn't realize. I just wanted to show you I am worthy of being your personal Lesser."

"So, you want to be my personal Lesser?"

"Yes, my God!"

Maxwell thought about it. "I will give it some thought. Meet me at 7:00pm in my room tomorrow," he said as he walked out of the room.

"Thank you, my God!"

The following day Elaine came knocking on Maxwell door at exactly 7:00pm.

"Ok, so you know a personal Lesser's job is to relay our messages and plans to the rest."

"Yes, and to take care of your needs," she said with confidence.

Maxwell exhaled. "I don't need anyone to care for me. I just need someone to do what I say to the letter and not disappoint me."

"Sorry for overstepping."

"As you know, there are some perks to being a personal Lesser. You have access to our fitness facility and our private room."

"To better be of service."

"Sure. Anyway, we will be doing a trial period."

"I will not fail you my God!" she said in excitement. "What would you need of me?"

"Didn't I just tell you I need nothing? You're an adult; figure it out," he said as he went back to work.

"Yes, my God."

Maxwell didn't really care about having a personal Lesser. He knew from his job at the firm that Lessers had a tendency to burn out when they pushed themselves too much, and he didn't want that to happen. He knew that she was capable, but he did not want to admit it a Lesser was capable, so he kept her on the side. She would come to his room and watch him work and even read. She was never late and never interrupted him. Just like he wanted. As time went by, he started noticing that he never had to put paper in the printer, his mini bar was always full, his steak was cooked just like he wanted, and there were new books on his bookshelf. He realized that she must have been watching him to learn his rituals and find out what he needed to make his life easier. He decided to give her a chance. He changed into his fitness outfit and called Elaine into his room.

"So, because of someone, work has been more seamless."

She smiled. "I'm just doing what needs done my God."

"Go change and follow me into my fitness center."

"Okay," she said as she went to get changed.

She met Maxwell in his personal fitness room, which wasn't different from the Lessers'.

Maxwell looked at her. "Give me a short idea of your workout."

She went on to show him what she normally did when working out, which was mostly weightlifting. Once she was done, she went back to Maxwell, staring him in the eyes that she couldn't get enough of waiting on his words.

"I noticed that you have been putting on more muscle lately. I'm guessing you changed your workout."

"Yes, since I don't work out as much, I switched to more weights so that I can be stronger for you, my God."

"On the contrary, for you I would recommend more speed. You've seen my sister. My brothers and I would think twice before getting into a fight with her, because she's so fast. It's like punching air. You lose energy and her punches always hit the mark. The next thing you know, you're on the floor."

"The Goddess is amazing. If I could do a fraction of what she can, that would be a blessing."

"So, from now on, make 70% of your workout cardio and 30% resistance."

"Thank you for taking the time to instruct me," she said as she smiled at him.

Maxwell felt uncomfortable as he kept looking at her smile; he has never felt the urge to genuinely give a Lesser advice, but here he was doing so.

"Since I have a lot on my plate, I figure I might as well have you help," he said, leaving the room with her in it. "Thank you for the books," he whispered under his voice.

Elaine didn't move. She first thought maybe she hadn't heard him correctly. Tears started running down her cheeks. She had long been wondering if he would notice the little things she was doing, if she was good enough to be a personal Lesser to a god. After all, she had always seen herself as a broken product. For the first time in a long time, she thought, *I'm not broken.*

As time went by, unbeknownst to Maxwell, he started to rely on her as more than a personal Lesser. He would talk to her about the selection of books that she had brought him. Even though he didn't notice the change in dynamic, his sister Myra did. At first, she paid it no mind. Normally they wouldn't associate with a Lesser, but because of the cream, it was a new world for him. One night Myra was one of the last to leave the facility, and she saw Maxwell picking up Elaine's keys that had fallen on the floor. The fact that Maxwell helped a Lesser was the trigger for her to be on watch. She knew that Maxwell would have never done that for a Lesser in the past. That's when she decided to put him to the test.

The following week, Myra called Elaine to her room. "How is my brother doing?"

"He is working hard, making sure that his facility work doesn't intervene with his personal work."

"That's good to hear." She walked toward Elaine. "Since he's been working so hard, I got him a gift. Would you mind picking it up for him?"

"It would be my pleasure!" she said excitedly.

"Great," Myra said with a smile. "It should be ready tonight at this location." She handed her a business card. "Once you pick it up, just deliver it to him."

"I will take care of it as if my life depended on it."

"Who said it doesn't?" Myra laughed "Just kidding. You'll be fine."

Elaine walked out in excitement. Now, she also wanted to get him something. She had some free time, since Myra had informed Maxwell that she would be borrowing Elaine for the day. She considered going to a bookstore and getting him a new book, but she wanted to get him a one that was different. Elaine looked around but couldn't find any book. She was about to give up when she saw one in the pile of used books. She picked it up. "Perfect, and right on time!"

She bought the book and headed to the pickup location. As she was driving by, she could tell it was a shady area, but she paid it no mind. She wanted to do this for him. Elaine got to the location, pulled into the parking lot and went inside to pick up the package. She got the package and headed back to her car when she saw a guy sitting on top of it.

"Sorry. Would you mind moving? That's my car."

The guy jumped off her car. "Of course not." He started walking toward her. "As long as you give me the package that you're holding." He pulled out a knife.

She froze. *No! This can't be happening again.*

Her hand started shaking. She looked at the man and then the box, then the shaking stopped. She put the box on the floor. She then moved it to the side using her feet. "Let me see you take it," she said to the man which sent him into a fit of rage. During the fight, she had the upper hand. She could see his attacks clear as day, and started thinking, this is what the Goddess must feel like. As she was moving around, she noticed that she was about to step on the box but caught herself in time. That gave the robber the time he needed to stab her in the stomach. She felt every inch of the knife going inside her and wanted to fall on the floor and curl up into a ball. She wanted to close her eyes but proceeded to grab the robber's hand, headbutting him.

The robber, seeing that she wasn't going down, yelled, "This is not worth it." and ran. As she watched the robber run away, she yelled, "Go back to your mama, you coward!" She looked down and could still see the knife in her. "Damn."

She winced as she picked up the package and walked back to her car. She didn't want to go back to the store, so as to not alert the police, and she wasn't in any condition to drive. She pulled out her phone and looked at Maxwell's number but hesitated to call. Elaine didn't want to waste his time on a Lesser like her, but she remembered she was doing it for the Goddess. She proceeded to send him a text, because she was worried that she couldn't keep her voice from cracking. She sat in the car for what seemed like forever and saw a car screeching into the parking lot. *I can finally close my eyes.* Maxwell was coming.

When she opened her eyes, she was at the facility laying on Maxwell's bed and unable to move. Next to her was Maxwell clenching his bloody fingers together.

"Are you hurt?" she asked, looking at his fingers.

"No, I'm fine. The better question is what took you so long to open your eyes?" he calmly stated with a smile.

"Sorry, I was having a nice dream."

"You were having a nice dream while-" he stopped himself from finishing the sentence.

"While?" she pushed.

Maxwell quickly changed the conversation, "What was your dream about?"

"I dreamt that this shadowy figure was crying, because he didn't want me to go. Saying that I had made him pick up the keys."

"That's a weird dream. I guess it's nice to be wanted."

She used what little energy she had to get up into a sitting position on the bed to better look at Maxwell and ask, "Am I wanted?"

Maxwell felt flustered. "You are in my room. My hands are covered in your blood from patching you up. My cheeks are wet from thinking about how mundane the world would be without you. You were wanted the moment I picked up your keys."

Tears started running down her cheeks as she moved her hand to hold his. "I don't want to wake up! If I wake up, I'll be back in the world where I'm broken."

Maxwell gently squeezed her hand until he could tell she was in pain. He got close to her ear and whispered, "Wouldn't you have woken already from the pain if this was a dream?" He let go of her hand.

While his face was close to hers, she could tell he had cried for her. Elaine smiled and put her forehead against his and whispered, "I guess even gods can cry."

"Who's crying?" he whispered back.

"That's the title of the book I got you. *When God Cried*." She giggled and got a bit closer to his lips. The closer she got to him, the more he could hear his own heartbeat. He also moved closer to her lips, until they could feel each other's breath. As their lips almost touched, Elaine turned her head away and told Maxwell, "I wish this was a dream, because that way I wouldn't be tainted. If only you hadn't woken me up."

Maxwell got up. "If I didn't wake you up, then I wouldn't be able to show you that you are not tainted. For now, get some rest. I need to speak to my sister."

"Going after Elaine?" Maxwell roared.

Myra looked at him with disregard and calmly walked to her minibar to pour herself a drink.

"If I didn't know better, I would say you're upset that I almost killed your personal. On the contrary, shouldn't you be upset that she got hurt with all the training we've given her?"

Maxwell felt like a fool. He had acted on his emotion—a dangerous thing to do in front of his sister.

"It's just annoying to find someone to replace her."

"Please! The four of us alone make enough money to pay for this whole operation. You work for a top investment firm, I'm a really expensive lawyer and our two brothers are the epitome of what a perfect human should look like. There are billions like her, but only twenty like us." She took a sip of her drink. "Did you get my gift?" she asked with a smile.

"Yes."

"Great, you can leave now. Oh! By the way, I hope she gets better soon. I really like her and wouldn't want to make the next time permanent."

Maxwell left his sister's room defeated, holding the knife that Elaine had risked her life for. He knew that it was a reminder that his sister wouldn't hesitate to kill him if he got in the way of the plan. He also knew that if his sister really wanted Elaine dead, she would already be dead. He just had to stay the course, and they would be fine.

A couple of months later, Elaine was back on her feet. There was some allure between Maxwell and Elaine at that point. The slight glance at each other, the gentle helping hand. Elaine found herself thinking of Maxwell more often than usual. Her God wanted her, she thought to herself with a smile, that was soon followed by sadness as another thought quickly followed: *I'm tainted.* She had convinced herself that what Maxwell wanted was the Elaine that was always there for him.

One night Maxwell arrived home after leaving the facility and thought to himself, *This house is so empty.* That thought was soon followed by an image of Elaine and him working together, and it struck him that he was genuinely smiling. It wasn't the fake smile that he would use at work or the smile that he had when he was with his siblings. It was a light smile where he didn't have to think of anything else. He laughed at himself, "I'm supposed to be better then them, and here I am acting like a coward. Soon, it's almost ready."

Two weeks had passed and both of them were working late like usual.

"I noticed you haven't read any books lately. Was the selection not to your liking?" she asked.

"No, I just had someone on my mind lately."

Don't ask him, she said to herself. "It must be an important person." *No! Why did you ask?*

"I think so. Actually, I'm going to need you to come with me tonight to meet them."

Why did it hurt when he said that? I should be happy to be able to spend time with him outside of the facility. "It would be a pleasure to meet someone important to you." she said, covering her feelings with a smile.

"Great." Maxwell handed Elaine the location for the meeting. "Just head there after you're done."

As Elaine watched Maxwell leave the room, her eyes lingered on him, hoping he would turn around and stay in their own little world. That moment ended when the door closed on her, and she was brought back to reality.

She rubbed her hands against her face. "What am I thinking?"

An hour passed since Maxwell had left, and Elaine was finally finished with her work. She got in her car and headed to the meeting location, all the while wondering who this person might be to her God.

She finally arrived at a big cabin outside the city. "Wow!" she said. She could never afford this place, especially since she gave most of her money to the facility. The door opened, and Maxwell came out. "I was beginning to think that you might have changed your mind."

She walked up to him. "I would never be absent from where you need me."

With a smile and a gentle voice, Maxwell said, " I see. You better keep that promise." He gave her his hand, inviting her in. She slowly slid her palm into his, gazing at his eyes. She felt a slight pressure from his hand, but she didn't mind. She knew she wouldn't regret seeing this side of him.

Maxwell felt flustered by her touch. He didn't want to let go of her hand and accidently gripped too hard. "Sorry."

"It's ok," she responded with a smile.

He guided her inside. "What do you think?"

The inside of the cabin was mostly white with ash grey floors which matched the wood lining on the ceiling. "It's definitely nicer than mine," she responded.

"I didn't know you also had a private cabin," Maxwell answered in all seriousness.

"Oh, yeah! I usually have to use my helicopter to get to it."

"On your salary?"

"I'm just joking," Elaine said as she realized that he was genuinely asking.

"Oh, I see."

They both started laughing at each other while still holding hands. Elaine had spent a lot of time with Maxwell, learning his habits and character, but this side of Maxwell was new to her, and she wanted more. For the first time, Elaine wasn't thinking of Maxwell as her God but the person she wanted to be next to. Maxwell wasn't thinking of Elaine as a Lesser but the person he wanted to be next to.

Maxwell continued the tour of the cabin and brought her to the dining room where there was food waiting for them on the table. "I figure you might be hungry after working so hard today."

"With you?" she asked him.

"I was hoping we could have dinner together, but if you want, I could eat outside. I like looking at the stars."

Why do I feel this way? Why does every second she takes to answer seem like a lifetime? Why am I clinging to her every word? Why do I feel so weak right now?

She started laughing. "It would be my pleasure to eat outside with you."

Maxwell smiled. "So, let's eat outside!"

Their hands tightened around each other before letting go. They both started making their own plate, until she noticed that most of the food on the table were her favorites. This whole time she thought she was the only one looking. She never realized that he was looking at her, seeing who she was and what she liked. She wondered if he wanted to see more of her as she wanted to see more of him.

After they had filled up their plates, Maxwell guided her back outside so they could have dinner on the patio. While Elaine was following him, he felt a tug on his shirt and stopped to turn.

"Don't turn! Please don't turn. I just need a second," Elaine said with a weak voice.

Maxwell waited a couple of seconds before breaking the silence. "I guess even a goddess can cry."

"That's not fair," she whispered back at him.

"You shouldn't be talking about fair."

"What do you mean?"

"Always staring back at me with that smile of yours. It's annoying that I started looking forward to seeing it."

"You're the cause of my smile." She gripped harder at his shirt. "Did you mean what you said that night?"

"What did I say?"

"That you would show me I'm not broken."

Without turning, Maxwell reached back and grabbed her hand. "Do you doubt my words?"

For a second she was taken aback by his words. "Of course not," she responded as she squeezed his hand harder. "Sorry if I'm hurting you."

"Did you say something?" he asked, feigning ignorance.

"No. Let's go eat."

They sat on the patio stairs for dinner. Once they were done, Maxwell washed the dishes and Elaine dried them. The last plate accidently slipped through Elaine's fingers and was about to hit the floor when Maxwell caught it.

"If this was a movie, the plate would have broken on the floor, and I would have tried picking it up and getting a cut on my finger and you with the way you love the scent of blood wouldn't-" She stopped herself from finishing that sentence, thinking, *what the hell am I thinking?*

Maxwell gazed at her and let go of the plate "Oops."

"Oops indeed." *What!* She screamed in her head.

As she went to pick up the pieces off the floor, Maxwell grabbed her hand. They gazed at each other and slowly moved closer. Elaine, remembering that night, thought, *maybe I truly am not tainted.* They could once again feel each other's breath upon their lips and just when they were about to kiss, Maxwell stopped and asked, "Would you mind following me?"

"Anywhere," she answered.

Maxwell took her hand and guided her to the basement. When they got there, Elaine saw a man tied up to a table.

"I told you I was going to show you you're not tainted." Maxwell let go of her hand and waited as Elaine walked toward the tied man.

As she got closer, she recognized him. She looked down at him and into his eyes. The man's mouth was taped shut. She didn't need to remove the tape to know that he didn't recognize her. She closed her eyes and thought about how much she had changed. Her past self would never have been able to get close to this lowlife. She had been trained at the facility by Maxwell; she had fought a robber with a knife and made him run away. Now, Maxwell gave her a knife.

Looking at Maxwell, she asked, " Can you help me?"

Maxwell nodded and from behind her, he grabbed the hand that was holding the knife. Together, they slowly raised it upward. "Goodbye to my old self," she said as they stabbed the man on the table. She let go of the knife and faced Maxwell and they let go of all the tension they were holding for each other that night.

They woke on the next morning near a puddle of blood and a dead body. As they were putting their clothes back on, Elaine stared at Maxwell and at the dead body on the table. "I guess my God is a knight."

Maxwell couldn't help but laugh.

"What's so funny?" she asked Maxwell.

Maxwell turned to face Elaine and grabbed her hand. "Hi, I'm Maxwell Knight. Would you like to spend the rest of your life with me?"

"Hi, I'm Elaine Dumfire and I would love to spend the rest of my life with you."

Chapter 8

A week had passed since the massacre. Richard and Alice were working overtime looking for suspects. Richard was at his desk going over everything for the hundredth time looking for something he might have missed when Alice came in.

"He's finally done!"

"What?"

"The coroner is done with the autopsies."

"Holy shit! I knew it was going to be quick but not that quick."

"He got some help to speed up the process."

"Then, what are we waiting for? 'Let's roll.'"

"Did you just say let's roll?"

"Hell, yeah, I did!"

"Why me?" Alice said exhaustedly.

The moment Richard saw the coroner, he couldn't help himself. "Hey, doc. What took so long?"

"Who knows? Could have been the thirteen dead bodies."

"He thinks he's funny when he's not. So, what do you have for us?" Alice interrupted.

"Well, if I could describe it in one word? Weird."

"How so?" she asked.

"Follow me." The doctor led them to a dead body without a head.

"So, what did he use to make this guy lose his head?" Richard smirked.

"On the report I put 'unknown' but between us I would say his hands for most of it."

Richard and Alice looked at each other, then at the body on the table.

"Super strong killer."

"Excuse me," the doctor intervened.

"Alice and I suggested this at the scene."

"Well, congratulations! I would say you hit the nail on the head."

Alice got close to the body. "You said most of it."

"What?"

"You said he used his hands for most of it."

"Oh, yeah, they apparently used a knife for some of it."

"But the head and arms that we saw didn't seem cut. Plus, a knife wouldn't be able to do that," Alice said, looking at the body.

"True. It seems that they used a knife to create a tear in the skin which would allow them to tear off the body part with sheer strength."

"What about when they didn't use a knife?"

"The head we found on the third-floor hallway was done with their bare hands. Two of them."

"Two of them?"

"One seemed to have been holding the body down while the other ripped the head off. There was a footprint on the back of the body and his sternum was cracked. Also, when we looked at the head there were even some finger indentations around the neck."

"Remind me to send you in first when we meet these criminals," Richard said looking at Alice. Ignoring Richard, she asked, "So, how many?"

"Okay, so from the 13 dead bodies, we found three sets of fingerprints."

"Are you sure it's three? Because I had money on four," Richard squinted.

"I said fingerprints, but we did find some strand of hair on the cleaning lady's uniform that didn't belong to her."

"So, four. Still got it!" Richard quickly responded.

"Was it only one woman?"

"I would say one woman and three men but that's just based on the fingerprints we found. There could have been more."

"Thank you, Doctor. That's good to know."

"Actually, Alice, I wanted to show you something." The doctor brought them to another dead body. Looking at Alice he asked, "Do you think you could have done this?"

Alice got close to the dead body and could see a fist indentation on its head. It was about half an inch deep.

"I can leave some bruises, but I can't do this and not many people can."

"That's what I thought."

Richard also got close to the body and looked at the indentation left on it. Alice was expecting him to say something funny, but all she could see on his face was a perplexing look.

"What's going through your mind?" she asked.

"Just thinking." He turned to face the doctor. "Do you have all the pictures in the file?"

"Yes." He pulled out a thick file and handed it to Richard.

Once they had looked at all the bodies and finished talking to the doctor, they went back to their work desk.

"That's a first for you."

"What do you mean?"

"That perplexed look on your face right now."

"Just something weird about the case."

"There's a lot of weird things about this case. We have four people that murdered twelve people and left a note behind."

"Those are minor things. A well-trained killer could easily achieve that. The weirdest thing to me is their relationship."

"I know what you mean. It doesn't make sense. I can see two of them working together, but those four are polar opposites. They could never work together like this."

"I was thinking the only way they could cooperate together would be if they're related."

"What are the odds of that?" she asked.

"I would normally say impossible, but now I'm not so sure. You know how rare it is to find a killer let alone two with similar style and two extra with different killing style." Richard turned to face Alice, "I'm not the only person with stuff on their mind. You've been thinking of something since you saw that body."

She exhaled. "When I saw those indentations left by the murderers, I wondered how much muscle they would need to do that kind of damage."

"A lot."

"Yeah, and that's the problem. You're telling me nobody saw a couple of muscle heads?"

"Unless they didn't look like muscle heads."

"You think a Nova might have been involved?"

"I did when I got to the scene, but I doubt it. There's not a lot of them in the city. They're always under the government's watch. Plus, there's only three Novas in the city, which means we would be missing a fourth."

"True. No one would miss the sight of some Novas. Plus, that would be too easy."

"True everything about this was planned, if they were Novas, they would have made it seemed like it was done by a regular human."

"So, we're dealing with people that are trying to frame Novas, maybe?"

"I don't think so. I think there's something we're not seeing yet."

"A hunch?" She asked.

"Something like that."

"Well, your hunches have a tendency of being right, so, let's hear it."

"Not yet."

"Why not?"

"It's too crazy. I want to confirm some things first," Richard responded as he looked at the note left by the murderers, his eyes fixating on the word EVO.

Alice changed the subject, annoyed that Richard wasn't sharing his thoughts. "Let's go over every detail."

"Sounds good."

Alice leaned against her desk, holding the file. "Let's start at the beginning. We know they must have prepared for this."

"They must have known the layout of the building before beginning."

"But when we looked at past recordings of the building, we didn't see anyone suspicious. Every person that was on the camera had an appointment. So how did they know where the elevator shutoff was located? And the router?"

Richard jumps off his desk. "The cleaning lady!"

"She knows the layout of the building and had access to the basement!"

"And they must have killed her to cover her track."

"Let's visit her place. I remember reading she has a roommate. There are too many dead bodies and families and friends to keep track of," she answered as she looked at the pile of files on her desk before leaving.

By the time they arrived at the apartment, the sun was already setting. As they were about to knock on the door, they heard a suspicious scuffle coming from inside. They pulled their guns out and Alice took a step back.

"It seems someone broke the door open." She kicked it, and Richard immediately ran in. There was no sound from the apartment as they roamed around looking for anything suspicious. As they were coming up to the last room, they heard the sound of glass breaking. Richard and Alice ran into the room to see a dead body on the bed and a man escaping through the fire escape. "Stop!" Richard yelled at the man who just ignored Richard and ran down the fire escape. "Damn!"

Richard ran after the assailant while Alice ran out of the apartment. Richard fired a shot and missed, but it slowed the assailant down. As the man made his way to the ground, Richard jumped, landing on a dumpster that was near the fire escape. Richard stood in front of the man on top of the dumpster and pointed his gun. "You just got dumped! Oh yeah!" He then jumped down from the dumpster. "What! Nothing? Sheesh, you need to get a sense of humor," he said as he got closer to the man. "Keep your hands up where I can see them and turn around."

As Richard was about to handcuff him. The man turned around and grabbed the hand holding the gun. Richard fired a shot, but it was too late, the man had turned the gun away from him. Richard was in shock and felt only a sharp pain in his jaw before he fell down on the ground. "You should really watch where you fall," the man said.

As he passed Richard, he felt a grip on his ankle, and next thing he knew, he was laying on the ground, too. "Touché," Richard said as he got up. His gun was under the dumpster, so he had to use his fists. A brawl ensued between the two men. Soon, Richard was being pushed back into a corner. *Crap! Because of this man, Alice is going to murder me with training,* Richard thought. Annoyed, Richard dodged the man's punch. "Do you know who my partner is?!" Richard said as he landed a flurry of punches on the man. Richard was able to finally take the man down when Alice showed up.

"Where were you?"

"Just watching the show," she said laughing. "'Do you know who my partner is!' Did you think you looked cool when you said that?"

Richard felt embarrassed, "So, you saw that?"

"Oh, yeah! And I will be seeing you at 5am for training tomorrow."

"Goddammit!"

As she was laughing, a man wearing a hoodie walked into the alleyway carrying a canister. Alice pulled out her gun. She couldn't see his face, because his head was facing the ground.

"Sir! There's an investigation going on. Please move away."

The man ignored Alice and kept walking toward them.

Alice pointed her gun at him. "Sir, do not move!"

Again, the man ignored her and kept walking toward them. She fired a warning shot near the man's feet. That's when the man dropped the container he was carrying and raised his head showing a silver mask covering half of his upper face. Alice could see the man's eyes through the mask, and immediately knew this was trouble. She fired her gun at him, but the man just kept dodging the bullets, staring her down.

Richard was in shock seeing the masked man dodging the bullets as he got closer to Alice. It took her a second to realize that the guy was looking at her gun barrel and finger to dodge the bullet. That second was too late, because the man was upon her. He landed a punch to her rib. Instinctively, she jumped back to decrease the effect of the blow. She instantly thought to herself, *This is one of them*, as she was sent flying.

Richard, still without a gun, rushed toward the masked man attempting to attack him. The masked man blocked every one of his hits. The man was toying with Richard, but he got bored quickly and smashed Richard's head into the concrete wall. It took Alice a minute to get up, trying to catch her breath. Alice could still feel the assailant's fist on her rib, but she pushed through the pain to get on her feet. In the time it took her to get up, the masked man had snapped the neck of the other assailant that Richard had arrested. Alice, seeing Richard passed out on the floor, attacked the masked man yet again. The man was dodging her attacks like they were nothing to him. He attacked Alice and was surprised to see her dodge his punch. "You're not the only one that can dance," she said as she threw a punch to the man's face, finally landing a hit. She wanted to unmask the man. She felt his strong grip on her wrist as he moved her fist away from his face, revealing his bright gray eyes. She knew those eyes. She'd had those eyes many times in the past when she was bored of her opponent. He was bored of her.

"Is that all?" the masked man asked.

Alice grabbed his wrist and the next thing he knew; he was on his knees while Alice pinned his hand to his back. "Do you know who you're messing with!?"

The mask man let out a laugh. "Actually, Alice, do you know who you are messing with?" He used his sheer strength to get off his knees. Alice tried to use all of her strength to keep him down but it was in vain. He rushed backward trying to slam Alice to the wall. Alice moved sideways and used his momentum to slam his face to the wall.

"This is for Richard!" Still on high alert, she saw the masked man move his hand and she quickly stepped back. The man cracked his neck, trying to show that he was just getting started.

"Okay! I felt that one." A smile appeared on his face. The man walked toward Alice "Let's try this again." He started a barrage of attacks on her. She was doing everything in her power to dodge every hit. She knew that one hit would be disastrous for her, and she wasn't at her full strength. She only had to hold on until Richard came to, but she was losing breath. She couldn't keep going as she was—but her hits, unlike his, were landing. She was enjoying herself. She started to slowly lose control as she got more and more into the fight, which gave the masked man the chance he needed to land a devastating hit to her rib a second time.

She fell to the ground, unable to move. The masked man sat on her, pinning her down, and pulled out a knife. He cut her palm and drained some of her blood into an empty vial. Barely able to keep her eyes open, she watched as the man walked to Richard and did the same to him. As the masked man was about to leave, he bent down near her. "Maybe next time, we can finish this dance." Then, he knocked her out.

The masked man walked to the container that was on the floor. "I hate how gasoline feels on my fingers."

He walked to the dead body on the floor and stepped on the man's mouth with all his might. He then set the body ablaze.

He left Richard and Alice passed out in the alleyway. As he moved away from the scene he threw the mask he was wearing in a trash can and made his way into another alleyway where a car was waiting for him.

"You took longer than expected," Myra said as she started the car. In the backseat, Ethan took his hoodie off. "She was better than I thought."

Myra handed Ethan a tissue. "I guess she was," she said with a smile.

"Why the tissue?"

"Your nose is bleeding."

Ethan had not realized that Alice broke his nose when she smashed his head on the wall. "Are you sure she doesn't have any Nova in her?"

"You saw her eyes."

"Yeah, I guess. I was just surprised. Have you ever killed one?"

"No, they're technically considered endangered so they tend to be guarded and hard to get to."

"True, plus most of them are famous. I wonder sometimes how their blood would smell."

"I can understand that feeling. If we're lucky, we might get to kill one at the end of this," she said, thinking about the person that might be hunting them down. Myra changed the subject. "I'm guessing you took care of the chaser?"

Ethan cleaned his bloody nose. "Yeah, when I got there Richard had already taken him down.""

"How was Richard?"

"He's definitely not on Alice's level, but he's better than our chaser. If I didn't knock him out early, I would have had to actually give it my all."

"A minute more and you would have been surrounded by a bunch of cops."

"That was the best part. The whole time I was wondering: was I going to make it or was I going to get caught? Honestly, I was waiting for her to say, 'Hey, aren't you that model?'" He smiled.

"I would have loved to see that."

"Maybe next time you'll get a front row seat, but in the meantime I got you a souvenir." Ethan pulled out two vials of blood. "Would you prefer Alice or Richard?"

"You should keep it for yourself. I want to be surprised when I drain them."

"Who knows? I might get to kill them before you do."

"Was it that fun that you would go against your loving sister? Makes me sad."

"You, sad. That would be the day."

"You don't think I can feel sadness?"

Ethan changed the subject " Do you think she will come?"

"She definitely will."

He hesitated. "To kill us?" He was scared of hearing the answer.

Myra nonchalantly answered, "Definitely to kill us."

"Is there any other outcome?"

"Well. You could keep hiding and spend the rest of your life wondering why you were thrown out, or we can force her to come out on our terms."

"I want to know."

"I know you do. We all do."

They entered a parking lot where there was just one car waiting. They got out of her car and James got out of his.

"What took you so long!?"

"Talk to our brother here, taking his sweet time."

"As an apology, you can have this." Ethan threw a vial of blood toward James.

James opened the vial and took a whiff. "That is actually really good." He raised his head and closed his eyes, enjoying the sweet smell. "I'm guessing they passed the test?"

Ethan pulled out the bloody tissue. "You guessed right."

"I want to be next!" James said. He closed the vial of blood, looking excited.

Myra, coming back from her car, handed them each a file. "You know what to do?"

"Of course."

"Great, I look forward to our next meeting." She got in her car and left.

Ethan looked at James. "Do you think she would mind if I went outside the plan a bit?"

"What do you think?"

Chapter 9

Richard lay in a hospital bed, finally able to open his eyes. He turned his head to see Alice sitting on a chair across from him.

"Well, this is embarrassing."

"You're telling me."

Alice squeezed her hand into a fist, and her cut reopened a bit. "He treated us like toys! He could have easily killed us," she said as she opened her fist and wiped the blood off.

Richard turned to face Alice and stared her down. "Don't worry. I will avenge us." They both started to laugh.

"Next time, we will both fight him together and make him regret ever toying with us."

"As long as we don't have to fight all four of them at the same time." Richard smirked.

As they were laughing at each other, Marc came rushing in. "I'm so happy you're all right!" he said as he squeezed and kissed Richard on the bed causing Richard to scream in pain.

"I'm not all right. He damaged my beautiful face and now you'll never love me." Richard pouted.

"Good thing I didn't love you for your face." Marc laughed.

Richard turned to face Alice. "He's just embarrassed to admit it."

"Look at you two being all lovey dovey." she smiled.

"Yeah, I have that effect on people."

"Oh! Shut up," Marc and Alice responded at the same time.

"Well, I am glad that you are having fun at my expense," he grumbled.

Marc turned to Alice. "For me, ignoring him works best sometimes."

"Oh, definitely! Sometimes I act like I'm listening when I'm not, and he actually keeps going."

"I know, right?! It never ends."

"Oh, my God! You should have heard him today, talking to our assailant. He actually said, 'Do you know who my partner is?' with so much confidence." Alice and Marc both started laughing.

"Okay, so this is definitely a nightmare." Richard rolled his eyes.

"Sorry, we're just joking."

"I'm the funny one of the group." Richard turns to Marc. "So, how upset are you?"

"Honestly it just hurts seeing you in this state. Maybe if you give me something to write about, I might feel better."

"Nice try!"

"Doesn't hurt to try."

Alice walked closer to Marc. "So, how much do you know?" she asked

"Well, I can guess that you both got hurt investigating the massacre. I can also guess that he got away. Am I missing something?"

"No, that's the gist of it."

"I do have one question for you."

"What is it?"

"Well, taking both of you down is not something just anybody can do. Was it by chance a Nova?"

"I didn't really get a look at his eyes," Richard responded.

"No, it wasn't. The culprit only had one color," Alice intervened

"Well, that will make the next piece much easier to write. Especially with who's running for mayoral office right now."

"Hey! Did you come here for me or to write a piece."

"I came for both!" He smiled as he kissed Richard.

Alice asked Marc if she could get a couple of minutes with Richard alone to which he happily complied. Alice took a deep breath and as she was exhaling, Richard beat her to what she was hesitant about saying. "They know who we are, don't they?"

Alice took a seat on Richard's bed. "Yeah. He even knew our names. How did you figure it out?"

"Well, those people are professionals and for some reason they left us a crumb, which they so happen to decide to get rid of on the day that we went to question the roommate. I don't believe in that much coincidence."

"That means we have a bigger problem."

"Yeah—a mole. That's the only way they would have known when and where we were going."

"This is annoying."

Richard smiled "This is actually perfect. If we can find the mole then we can find them."

"True."

"By the way, where's your husband?"

"I told him I was all right and that you were the one that was hurt."

"Wow! He doesn't even show up to see how I'm doing. So selfish."

"Oh! I'm so sorry; I'll have a talk with him about that."

Richard stared at Alice "Speaking of...How badly are you hurt?"

Alice raised her shirt up, showing her stomach and bruised rib.

"How are you even up?"

"It doesn't hurt as much as my pride."

"Why didn't you have the doctor use the nice Teltius tech we fought for to heal you?"

"I want to remember this feeling."

"People lose sometimes. It happens."

"It was the way I lost. He could have easily killed us, especially you. Those culprits have crushed skulls with their fists. Why didn't they do it to you or me?"

"They want us alive for something."

"Well, I don't like being toyed with," she mumbled.

Richard was able to get discharged a couple minutes afterwards. It had been four hours since the incident happened, and they were ready to go back to the scene of the crime. Since they had left their car at the scene, they asked Marc for a ride. Marc was against it at first mostly because he was worried about him, but Richard and Alice were able to convince him to help.

They finally made it back to where it had happened, the cleaning lady's apartment.

"The door was locked when we arrived. So, I guess the man either had the keys or was even welcomed in."

"Why would the roommate welcome him in?"

"Maybe he said he had some information about the cleaning lady."

"I guess."

They went into the room that the culprit escaped from. Richard looked at the bed where the body had previously lain. The coroner had since taken it away. "Smart not using a gun. Less ways for us to track them."

"Actually, so far there's been no sign of a gun at any of the scenes." Alice turned to Richard. "How was the guy that you chased down the fire escape?"

"Honestly? Better than the average criminal. If it had been someone else, they would have lost."

"So, they were trained to fight without a gun. Makes me wonder if they did not use a gun because it doesn't call for it or because that's not what they believe."

"Well, there's no one to ask at the moment," Richard said, before his knees buckled under his weight. He grabbed the dresser to stop his fall. Alice rushed to him, "Are you all right?"

"Yeah, just my head."

"Why didn't you let the doctor heal you?"

"If my partner isn't using those damn Teltius tech, neither will I."

"You should have at least gone home to rest. I can handle this by myself."

"Would you have?"

Alice smiled. "I guess not."

"Can you check the dresser? I heard something move when I grabbed hold of it."

Alice moved the dresser and saw an envelope on the floor. She picked it up and opened it. She showed the open envelope to him. "That's all she got?"

"Well, I'm guessing if she knew she was going to get killed she would have asked for more money."

Alice handed the envelope to an officer to be entered into evidence. As the officer left, Alice glared at his back.

"Stop glaring. I doubt he's the one and if he is, he won't confess by you just glaring."

She walked back to Richard. "Sorry, it just pisses me off thinking that anyone here could be the mole."

"Actually, I'm happy we have one."

"Excuse me."

"Think about it. If we can find the traitor, then everything will unravel itself."

"I guess if you look at it that way…"

"Plus, if they keep monitoring us, we will most likely meet that guy again."

She smiled. "Try not to get knocked out next time."

"I'm not going to live that down, am I?

"Don't you know who my partner is?" She joked.

"Okay, okay, I get it."

They searched the apartment before revisiting the alleyway. The charcoaled body was lying on the floor with the crime scene examiner taking pictures.

"How upset do you think the boss will be about this?" He asked Alice.

"Well, he's been on us to solve this case, because the mayor has been putting pressure on."

"So, not so upset." He smirked.

"Of course not. That's why you should do the honors and tell him how we let the only suspect escape."

"I'm a humble man. I would rather you have the credit for that."

"Sure, I won't mind telling him how you fell asleep during the interaction," she said, as she left him behind to look at the body.

"I guess they didn't want us to figure who this was."

"They burned and crushed his mouth. So, we have nothing to go with. Hopefully his DNA is in the database," the medical examiner answered.

"I doubt it." She turned to Richard, who was staring at his phone outside the alleyway. "What are you doing?"

"I figure it's a waste to look for clues here. Leave that to the crime scene investigator for now. Let's follow the masked man."

"I doubt we're going to find him at this point."

"I doubt that also," he said, leaving the scene.

Alice followed him. "How do you know he went this way?"

"I used my phone to search for stores in the area. I noticed there was a store in the opposite direction and most likely they have a camera on the outside. So, assuming they're not stupid they would have gone the opposite direction."

"We should still send an officer to go get the footage from that store."

"Already did," he answered.

As soon as they came to the end of the block, she looked into the trash can.

"What are you looking for?"

"It might be nighttime, but someone walking with a mask at night would still be suspicious especially after hearing multiple gun shots."

"You think he got rid of it?"

"I hope he did 'cause otherwise I'm just embarrassing myself. Just not in this trash can, it seems."

Richard kept looking at his phone going in the opposite direction of any location that might have cameras outside, while Alice searched the trash cans. She finally found the mask two blocks into her search.

"I thought something was off." She handed the mask to a gloved Richard.

"What do you mean?"

"The fact that I couldn't unmask him was weird."

"So, a sturdy metal mask. Hopefully there is some DNA on it that we can add to the database."

"True. Let's keep walking," she said as she bagged the mask.

They walked for a couple more blocks until they reached another alleyway.

"And that's where he had a car waiting for him." Richard pointed.

"How do you figure?"

"This is the only location without a camera, a blind spot, if you will. There's a camera at the end of the block, too."

"So, was there someone waiting for him? Or was it an empty car?"

"What if instead of just waiting, the person drove around until it was time to pick him up?"

Alice smiled. "Do you think we might have them on camera?"

"There's only one way out of this alleyway, which leads to a one-way street. What do you think?"

"We got you." She smiled.

Richard punched Alice's arm. "What's going on with you?" he asked.

"What do you mean?"

"I just feel that you've been acting differently since this incident."

"I just had something on my mind."

Richard took a second to think. "You remember at

the precinct when I told you I had a hunch but wanted to confirm it before saying anything?"

"What about it?"

"Well, I think I might have confirmed it."

"What is it?" She asked in anticipation.

"I might be crazy thinking this, but I've been stuck on the name 'EVO'. At first I wondered if it was an acronym for something, but what if it means what they say?"

"Evolution?"

"Right! That's the first word that came to mind. So, what if they're a group of people who believe they're the next evolutionary step to humanity?"

"I would say that's possible."

Richard was in shock from Alice's response. "What really?! I guess we got hit pretty hard in the head."

"Before being killed, the assailant said something to the masked man."

"What did he say?"

"'Thank you, my God.'"

Chapter 10

Alice woke up later than usual, skipping the gym in order to heal as fast as possible. She didn't know when she would have to confront the masked man again, but she vowed to be ready. Alice put the television on as she prepared to leave for the precinct. Phillip had already left for work, unaware of what had happened the night prior.

Alice had the house to herself for another forty minutes, so she leisurely finished her breakfast and sat on the couch, thinking. She could not believe that one of the culprits was in front of her and she couldn't stop him. Worst of all, they let him kill the only lead they had. As if it was reading her mind, the morning show started discussing the altercation. Her eyes widened as she listened to the host.

"Last night two detectives made contact with one of the suspected killers from the massacre that happened weeks ago, and they just let him go. I thought their job was to protect but they couldn't even do that. It appeared that the killer didn't just get away, but also managed to kill an assailant the detectives were in the process of arresting."

The news kept going on about how bad the police force was. As she and Richard got attacked by the media, her phone started ringing.

"Are you watching it?!" Richard yelled.

Alice frustrated answered, "You know, I just wanted to take it easy, and this is what happens."

"How the hell did they get that information?!"

"I'm guessing Marc hasn't written his piece yet."

"He hasn't. Plus, he wouldn't hit us like that."

"I know. Sorry, I'm just frustrated right now. Can you have Marc look into how these reporters got their information?"

"I'll ask. Hopefully he'll be able to find something."

"Do you think the captain saw this?"

"Well, I just got a missed call from him right before calling you. My advice? If he calls, don't answer the phone."

"I think I'll take that advice."

"I'll see you at work."

"See you."

Shortly after, her phone rang with the captain's name on the screen. She ignored it, knowing the reason he was calling. She didn't want to deal with this over the phone. It was time for her to head out. She got into her car, put on some music, and went to work.

That very morning Richard had been awakened by his cats stepping on his face. That was their way of saying they were hungry.

"Oh, my God. You guys aren't going to die if you give me just thirty more minutes!"

Marc turned around. "Well, I guess we're up now. Thank you," he said, glaring at Richard.

Richard, still laying in bed said. "I can't help but feel that you're blaming me for this."

"Well you're the one that woke me up, not the cats."

"Of course. Siding with them."

Richard got off the bed and went to feed the starving cats, meowing at him nonstop until their bowls were full. Marc also got up and started getting ready for work. As they were done getting ready, Marc started making breakfast. He didn't want Richard to push himself too much after what happened last night. Richard made some coffee and began pouring sugar in.

"I think that's enough," Marc remarked.

"What?"

"You need to cut your sugar."

"But I need this! It brings me joy." He grinned.

"Well, I need you to be safe and healthy. I can't do anything about the safe part, but I can do something about the healthy part," Marc said as he got close to Richard and kissed him.

"Oh, that's tricky."

"What? I'm just giving you a better kind of sugar." Marc flirted.

"How can I say no to that?" Richard flirted back as they kissed.

As they sat down to enjoy their breakfast, Marc got an email on his phone. His eyes widened as he read it.

"Are you kidding me?!" He said as he ran to the television. He turned on the news channel to see a newscaster talking about the events from last night. Richard walked up to Marc.

"I'm guessing that's not your piece?"

"No! Apparently after I submitted my piece last night, another reporter gave them a more detailed piece of last night's event!"

"That would explain why this newscaster is making us look bad."

"I'm sorry."

"Don't be."

"Are you going to be in trouble?"

"Yep. It's bad when we mess up but even worse when the news gets the information out to the public."

Just as Richard finished his phone rang. It was his captain calling.

"Speaking of the devil." Richard said as he looked at his phone.

"I'm guessing he's watching this also."

"I need to call Alice before the captain does."

After Richard finished his conversation with Alice. He turned to Marc. "I'm going to need a favor."

"What is it?"

"Could you look into who got that information out before you?"

"It should be pretty easy."

"Thanks."

Richard, like always, went to the small coffee shop only to see Alice waiting for him outside. "What are you doing here?!"

"Well, if we are going to get yelled at, we might as well do it as a team." She smiled

"True." They went into the coffee shop, and both ordered a cup. "Extra caramel please."

"Do not put any extra caramel in his cup." Alice cut in.

"Excuse me?!"

Alice turned to Richard with a smirk. "Marc texted me this morning."

"Oh! He did?" Richard sounded surprised. "Did I say extra caramel? I meant the regular amount."

"That's what I thought."

As they were walking to the precinct sipping on their coffee, Alice had to ask. "Do you think they already requested the National Crime Investigation Unit to intervene?"

"I would be surprised if they hadn't. Especially with a mayoral election happening right now."

"Actually, Phillip was talking about it a couple nights ago. Supposedly this is a big one. It's the first time a Nova is running for election."

"The irony. We are currently helping the Teltius that wiped out Novaria and now a Nova is trying to become a political leader."

"She probably would be better than our current

mayor who thinks he can just snap his fingers and magically resolve everything."

"You shouldn't let the mayor hear that. He might get upset." Richard laughed.

As they walked to their desks, Richard and Alice could see the captain in his office waving them in. They looked at each other. "Well, time to get it, I guess," Richard said, grimacing.

They walked into their captain's office.

"Would you mind closing the door?" their captain asked. "So, how are you two doing after last night?"

"Honestly? A little pain here and there, but nothing that will stop our investigation."

"My head is killing me, but, like she said, nothing that will keep us down."

"I thought it must have been pretty bad for you not to pick up your phone."

"Sorry—we were working late last night, and I got up late and was rushing to get to work." Richard fumbled over his words.

Alice looked at Richard and back at her captain. "Yes, after last night I wanted to be able to recover as much as possible and woke up late."

"Do you know who's not waking up late? The press

isn't waking up late. The mayor isn't waking up late," the captain said, with a stern look. Richard and Alice knew that he wanted to yell at them but was trying to keep it in.

"I take it that you saw the news," Richard said as Alice slapped his leg trying to tell him to be quiet.

"Not only me. The mayor saw it, and unlike you, I can't just ignore a call from the mayor until I'm ready to deal with it." The captain exhaled and took a couple of breaths, trying to remain calm. "Honestly, you two are my best officers, well, one of you, and I know that given time you can solve this, but the mayor is not giving us time. He has requested the NCIU to take the lead on this case."

"Sir, I don't think that's a good idea. Inviting the NCIU in at this point would be playing a catch-up game," Alice said with concern.

"Plus, they're a bit self-centered," Richard added.

"Really?" both Alice and the captain said at the same time, looking at Richard.

"Okay, message received," Richard said, backing off.

"Honestly, the mayor doesn't care about getting this done quickly," the captain said bringing the conversation back.

"So, why?"

"He wants to blame this on a group of Novas," the captain replied.

"But we have no evidence that any Nova was involved," said Alice.

"He wants to damage the reputation of the Novas to make the election easier to win," Annoyed Richard responded, realizing the mayor was using them for his agenda.

"Yeah. I already told him that in your report from last night, there was no sign of Nova involvement."

"So, he is bringing outside people that will agree with him. Politicians!" Alice growled.

"Honestly after reading your report, I wondered if a Nova was involved."

"I saw the masked guy's eyes. Both of them were bright gray."

"It doesn't matter. Just stick with what you wrote on the report. If the NCIU disagrees, that will be on them in the future."

"So, when are we going to their office?" Alice asked.

"You both are heading there tomorrow."

"Do you know who will be in charge?"

"You will be reporting to Agent Troy."

"So we have one day to solve this. Time for me too shine!" Richard joked.

"I will need you to prepare everything that you currently have to present to them when you arrive."

"Will do," Alice and Richard responded.

They left the captain's office and went back to their desk.

"Honestly, I would prefer if he had yelled at us."

"I would prefer if the mayor didn't interfere with the investigation and turn it into a political plot," Alice responded angrily.

"You really don't like him."

"I just don't like that he's abusing his power and isn't even hiding it."

"Maybe we should leak that information to the Nova running for mayor."

"The NCIU will have her in their line of sight and if we leak that information to her, we will also become targets. If she wants to be mayor, she will have to learn how to deal with this."

"I guess you don't like anyone running for office."

"Anyway, how are we going to deal with the NCIU?" she asked, trying to change the conversation.

"I think we should cooperate with them and support them."

They both looked at each other and started laughing.

"So, we'll be doing our own investigation on the side?" Alice smiled.

Alice's phone rang. She looked at it and smiled.

"I guess the husband is calling."

"I'll be back," she said as she answered her phone and walked away. "Hi, I missed you last night. Sorry I came home late."

"I missed you last night, too. Are you okay?"

"Of course, darling. Why do you ask?"

"I saw the news. They were talking about you."

"Don't worry. I'm famous now, that's all."

"I just want to make sure that you're all right."

"It's part of the job. I didn't mention it because I didn't want to worry you. We can talk about it tonight. How does that sound?"

"I guess I have no choice."

"You know that I love you right?"

"And you know that I love you."

"Can't wait to see you tonight."

"I feel the same. Bye, my love."

"Bye sweetheart," she said as she hung up and went back to her desk.

Richard couldn't help himself. "How romantic! Your husband called to check on you."

"I know! It's just as romantic as Marc coming to see you in the hospital," she teased Richard

"Touché."

As they were preparing the files for the NCIU team, an officer walked up to them. "We were able to collect all the videos of the stores in the neighborhood. We set everything up in the video room."

Alice jumped up. "That's fantastic! Thank you."

In the video room, they were greeted by an officer waiting for them to start.

"I think we should start with the one closest to where he might have had a car waiting," Richard said to the officer.

"Are you sure you don't want to see the one closest to the attack?" The officer asked.

"He won't be on those videos. There's only one video he will be on and it's the one by the alley," Richard answered before turning to Alice. "At least I hope so."

"We believe that he got into a car and since the alleyway leads to a one-way street we should be able to see it," Alice said as she put her hand on the desk.

They started watching the recording which came from the local corner deli. They knew the perpetrators had to appear on the camera.

"What about this car?" The officer pointed.

"No, not that one," Alice answered.

"But they're going over the speed limit like they're trying to escape."

"Or they just had to use the bathroom. We are dealing with people that plan everything and kill individuals without batting an eye. They would be complying with all traffic laws."
The trio stared at the screen in anticipation.

"Stop! Here!" Richard yelled. There were three cars on the screen and Richard pointed at the red car. "That's the one."

"Why that one?" Alice asked Richard.

"We have three cars. Two are in the left lane while the third is on the right, leaving the middle lane empty. The car on the right is turning."

Alice looked at the screen for a second. "I see. The car on the right is obviously turning; which leaves either the blue car in the front or the red car behind it. "

"Exactly! Plus, the car on the right has one person in it."

"Ok but why the red?" The officer asked yet again.

"You have three car lanes but only two are being used. So, why is the red car behind the blue when it could be in the middle. Because they didn't want to be seen by the other driver," Richard answered with confidence.

"Plus, the timeline matches, and the red car has two people in it. Can you zoom in on the license plate?" Alice asked as she waited to write down the license number.

"So, should I stop?" The officer asked.

"No, let's watch the next twenty minutes. Just to make sure and also look up the license plate of the other cars to be on the safe side."

"You think they might have waited in the alleyway for that long?"

"You never know; plus, we can remove that possibility."

"I guess."

After they were done, the only suspicious car they had found was the red one. Alice and Richard went back to their desks while Alice went on her computer and looked up the license plate.

"All right! Found the address of the car owner. Johnathon Witmore. Age 40. Currently unemployed. Married to a May Witmore."

"Let's take my car and head out there."

"We are taking my car."

"No, I want to drive."

"Then get a better car," Alice stated.

"What's wrong with my car?"

"How do I say this? It's a piece of crap."

"Hey, it drives from point A to point B."

"I can't believe these words came out of your mouth. All right, let's flip a coin for it." Alice pulled out her lucky coin from her pocket.

Alice drove to the address and got out of her car with a smile. "Driving always feels relaxing."

Richard came out of the car annoyed. "I know you cheated."

"Don't think about it. We're here now and that's what matters."

"Sure."

As they were walking up to the house, Alice noticed that there was no car parked in the driveway.

"Here's hoping the owner is home." She knocked on the door. After a couple of seconds, a woman opened it. Alice and Richard introduced themselves to the woman and informed her that they were detectives investigating a case. She invited them in.

"Is your husband home?"

"No, he's at work right now."

"I thought he didn't have a job," Alice questioned her.

"I'm sorry; it's not something we like to bring up in conversation. He's out looking for work, currently."

"I understand. I'll get straight to the point. During our investigation, we noticed your car driving around the area of the incident. Two nights ago. Could you tell us how that came to be?"

"Oh. I don't remember passing by any crime scene or seeing any police. We were thinking of going to a restaurant to cheer up, but my husband didn't feel well, so we drove back."

Richard walked into the living room looking at the pictures. "So, your husband is feeling better?"

"Yes, it was just a stomach bug."

Richard saw a gold sculpture in the shape of an eye. The pupil was two gems fused together: blue and pink. Richard quickly noticed that the sculpture's stand had a secret compartment "You're a Nova worshipper?"

The lady stood up and walked toward the sculpture. "We used to be worshippers, but not anymore."

"What changed?" Alice asked.

"They never answered."

"What would have happened if they did?"

The lady smiled. "It would give meaning to the hours, the days, the years I spent praying to them."

Alice stared her down. "Would you die for them?"

"Wouldn't you die for your gods?"

"Sorry. Not a believer."

"Too bad. You might change your mind in the future," the lady answered as she walked to her front door and opened it, signaling them it was time to leave.

As Alice was leaving, she said, "I thought you said you weren't a worshipper?"

The lady smiled at Alice and Richard. "I guess deep down you never stop."

Chapter 11

The following day, Alice and Richard reported to the NCIU. The moment they entered the building, they could tell it was different from their precinct clean and empty. The few people they saw were impeccably dressed and focused on what they were doing to give them the time of day.

"Much cleaner than ours?"

"Well, they're the second most powerful government agency after the military. What do you expect?"

Richard exhales, "Well, let's do this."

After passing security, they were instructed to go to the fourth floor where agent Troy's office was located.

The fourth floor looked futuristic, with clear glass walls surrounding Richard and Alice. A dark wall turned transparent in front of their eyes as people started coming out of the room.

"Did the glass change color?!" Richard exclaimed.

"Okay. We need to get that."

An agent passed by Alice and Richard and snickered.

"Did he just snicker at us?!"

"It's the NCIU attitude. We'll have to get used to it. We can't make the captain look bad."

"I guess."

They ignored the man and kept walking until they reached Troy's office, where the door opened automatically for them. They walked in to see a man working on his computer.

"Hi, we are—"

Before Richard could finish, Troy cut him off. "I know who you are, so let's move on. I have read the case. I would like to know why you do not believe a Nova was involved," he asked.

Richard, annoyed, finished, "Here to report for the investigation."

"Honestly, I don't really care who you are. Normally we only deal with national crime. We are doing this investigation to give some face to the mayor. He believes this was done by a couple of Novas, but you seem to disagree. And since you're detectives on the case I would like to know why." All the while he kept working on his computer without lifting his eyes.

Alice put her hand in front of Richard as her way of telling him to calm down. "In the report, I said we currently have no reason to believe a Nova was involved. They are peaceful people."

"Peaceful people. Ha! I guess you've never seen a Nova that was raised in Menea."

Alice ignored him and kept talking. "As there was no evidence, there is no reason to speculate the involvement of Novas."

"I see why the mayor requested our help with this case," Troy responded as he got up. "We will be going to the briefing room where the rest of my team are waiting for us. Please don't mention your ideas to them." He left the room signaling them to follow.

Alice and Richard looked at each other in annoyance. They hated the NCIU's tendency to focus on foreigners as their primary culprit. As they followed Troy, he showed them their desks. It was a small room where two people were already inside working. They kept following Troy into a see-through glass room where three more people were sitting at a table. As Troy closed the door, the glass room turned dark. Nobody introduced themselves or even paid much attention to Alice and Richard. Troy took a seat and inserted a flash drive in the hollowed table. A holographic image appeared in the center of the table and the same imagery projected on the table in front of each person present.

"So, 13 victims were murdered. Out of the 13, one was the female janitor and the rest worked for a small marketing firm located inside the building. So far, the police have nothing and requested our intervention." Troy touched his table screen and the center hologram focused on the cleaning lady Laureen, displaying all her information. "She is the only connection we have to the murderers. Her roommate was murdered in front of our detectives here. Then they watched as the culprit got killed by a masked assailant that apparently left both detectives incapacitated as he fled the scene."

Everyone in the room looked at Alice and Richard.

"Piece of shit," Richard whispered under his breath.

"We don't have any information about the assailant, but we do know they were driving this red car." Troy touched the screen and a red car appeared in the center. "We are bringing the couple in and searching their house."

"Must be nice to not need a warrant," Richard said sarcastically.

"Actually, it's nice when you're capable," Troy responded, which caused the room to snicker at Richard and Alice. "We know that the couple used to be worshippers of Novas in the past. As we all know, we currently have three Novas in the city, which puts Neveah Orcus and her two bodyguards at the top of our list."

"Wait! You can't just put every Nova in the city on the list!" Alice interjected.

"I wouldn't have to if you both hadn't let our main suspect escape."

"Okay, yes he escaped. But he wasn't a Nova."

"That doesn't mean the rest aren't Novas. Maybe they sent that guy after you to deter the idea that it was a Nova. Actually the more I say it, the more I'm certain a Nova is involved. Perhaps you're a Menea supporter. You're a fighter, aren't you?" Troy said in the hope of rattling Alice.

"Hey!" Richard yelled.

Alice cut him off. "In my two-year mandatory military service, I was sent to the field and my team came face to face with a Menean soldier. It took a team of six to take that monster down. That was the first time I realized how weak I was, and I made sure to get stronger. But you, I can tell, have never faced one of those monsters—and even worse, have never stared down a Nova from Menea. Because if you had, they would be the last thing you would want to come face to face with," she responded in a calm manner.

"Yes, I remember reading that in your file. It's funny how a deserter is questioning my courage."

Alice banged the table and stood up. "How dare you!"

An agent walked in. "Sir, the suspect is waiting to be questioned."

"Great, we will be there in a bit," Troy responded. "All right, let's go question the couple. Oh! I forgot. We have some call logs that we got from the couple; would you mind double-checking the information? It would be a shame if we miss something," Troy said to Alice and Richard

"I think we should participate in the interview. We already spoke to the wife." Alice countered.

"Last time I checked, I'm in charge and I decide what is important."

"Don't worry; we will gladly take care of it" Richard smiled as Troy left them behind.

When Alice and Richard got to their work desk, they introduced themself to the two other detectives, that were in the same room as them.

"So, this is where they put the police help," Richard said sarcastically.

"Yeah, they seem to think we get in the way," one of the detectives answered.

"I kind of gather that," Alice added.
As they were getting to know each other, a man walked into the room.

"Alice, is that you?"

"Adam! You're still at the NCIU?"

"Well, yeah. What about you still with the police?" Adam asked.

"Where else would I be?" she responded.

"Here, with us."

"No, thank you," she quickly responded.

"Ahem," Richard cleared his throat.

"Oh! This is my partner, Richard."

"Hi! I'm Adam, nice to meet you," he responded as he shook Richard's hand.

"The pleasure is all mine," Richard replied with a wink.

"Ooookay. So, why are you two here?" Adam asked, looking at Alice.

"We are here to help Troy with the massacre investigation. He needs our help and is currently stumped," Richard intervened.

"You guys are working with Troy. I'm sorry in advance. He's a bit more hardline."

"He's not the only one," Alice responded.

"Well, this job does that to you."

"Even you?" She asked.

Adam took a second and looked at her. "We saw the same thing that day and you even more so, so it's hard not to be defensive. Sorry, I have to go. It was nice seeing you again, and nice to meet you, Richard."

As Richard watched Adam leave, Alice couldn't help herself. " I wonder what I'm going to have to tell Marc when I see him."

"Nothing, that's what. Was he trying to recruit you?"

"Well, I'm not interested."

"I know that, but how come he didn't try to recruit me?"

"I could think of a couple of reasons."

"Yeah! Jealousy."

"Exactly what I was thinking," Alice responded with a smile.

They went back to work on the case but didn't feel comfortable talking about it in front of another team of detectives. Richard and Alice decided to find a location where they could be alone. They finally found an empty staircase. Richard took a seat while Alice paced.

"So, are we actually dealing with a cult? That statue at the Witmore's and, the fact the culprit said, 'thank you, my God', before being killed."

"That's the only way to convince someone to die for you. By making them believe in something greater than themselves," Richard elaborated.

"The couple is definitely connected to this case."

"I have a feeling they won't let us interview them," Alice responded with frustration.

"Well, it doesn't matter anyway. If they're willing to die for their cause, they won't say anything."

"Maybe if we added enough pressure, they might slip."

"I doubt it," Richard said while tilting his head upward to see if anyone was coming and continued. "That couple were worshippers for years and they suddenly stopped worshipping. What if they found a greater purpose? What if someone answered their prayers for once? What do you think would happen?"

"They would sacrifice everything for that person. So, what kind of person could answer those prayers?"

"If a non-Nova came out of nowhere and displayed Nova characteristics, like super strength, wouldn't you want to follow that person? Wouldn't a part of you wonder if you could gain that strength?"

"That's impossible. Novas are the only humans that have super strength."

"I know, but the way those dead body were ripped apart, the way that guy took us down... He dodged bullets."

"So, there's a group of non-Novas that has super strength?"

"That would be my best guess. Crazy right?" Richard responded.

"I know they experimented on Novas in the past trying to figure out why they are freakishly strong, but they were always unsuccessful."

"What if they succeeded?"

"Even if they did, what would be the point of the massacre?"

"Well, they could have gone rogue."

"That doesn't make sense."

"Well, I don't have all the answers."

Alice took a deep breath. "Okay, so we know that everything that has happened so far has been planned. I would assume that they knew we would figure out that the couple is part of this somehow. So, what's not part of the plan?"

Richard stood up. "You said with certainty that the man that attacked us was one of the four killers?"

"Without a doubt. Why else would the guy call him 'God'."

"How do you think the murderers would feel if all of the focus was switched to them being Novas?"

"You think they would be upset?"

"Think about it. This is not their first kill, so they must have been killing before and we just didn't know about it. So, why do something so big if you've been killing secretly?"

Alice smiled. "Because you want to be noticed."

"Exactly. So, when the NCIU goes public with the story that a Nova is involved, it will hopefully piss them off enough for them to reveal themselves."

"Let's hope it happens soon."

"By the way, why did you say you were a deserter?"

Alice exhaled. "Do you really want to know?"

"Yes, you're my partner."

"I don't like talking about it but here goes. When I was in the army my team met with two Novas from Menean. We were cocky after taking out the Menean soldiers. We figured the Novas were just hyped up; they couldn't actually be super strong, but they were. They decimated us. I watched everyone on my team get killed."

"But you made it."

"Barely. I can still remember the moment when I realized I was going to die. I was bloody beaten senseless, because I wouldn't give up and he came."

"Who?"

"An old man." Alice laughed. "He saved me and taught me for a year how to defend myself."

"And that year that you were gone, they tagged you as a deserter."

"Yeah, when I came back, I was considered a deserter. There were a lot of deserters, especially with rumors of Darius joining the battlefield."

"If I heard the strongest Nova on the planet was in the area, I would run, too."   "It took everything for me to remove the label of being a deserter. I had to work twice as hard, put my life on the line more times than I can count all so that the Teltius can give us a scrap of their technology. We fight a war that's not even ours so that we can live a little longer." Alice growled as she hit the wall.

"You won't hear any argument from me when it comes to this stupid war."

"The worst part is that they glorify it. They make it seem like it's for the greater good, but when I was on the field, there wasn't a single Teltius there. It was just our people and the Mencan killing each other."

"I'm sorry you had to go through all that." Richard said as he lightly punched Alice in the shoulder. "Good thing you have me to cheer you up."

"Sorry, but Phillip beat you to it." She smiled.

"I definitely can't beat him, but, hey, I'm a close second."

"It's between you and Marc." She laughed as they went back to their desk.

That night Richard went home to find Marc waiting for him. He had already made dinner having finished work earlier than Richard.

"Something looks tasty."

"Well, you'll have to wait after dinner to have some."

"I guess I'll need to finish eating as quickly as possible," Richard said as a gently pulled Marc in, kissing him.

"So, how was your day?" Mark asked, switching the subject.

"It could have been better. How about yours?"

"Well, I tried finding the person that leaked the information to the press before me, but I've got nothing yet. More like my boss is not telling me who gave him the information."

"Well, I didn't think it was going to be easy."

"Do you think the person that provided the information could be involved in the case?"

"There was no one else in the alleyway, but the information that was given was perfectly accurate. The only other person that had that information is the captain and I don't think he leaked that information out."

"I'll keep searching."

"Thanks," Richard responded with a kiss.

After they were done eating dinner, Marc and Richard sat together, leaning on each other while watching tv with one cat on Marc's lap. Richard interrupted.

"You made dinner. Can't help but feel that you wanted to question me, so come out with it."

"Okay, so how was the NCIU?" Marc jumped off the couch and started questioning Richard.

"That was fast... to be honest, bad. They're single-minded and only see one option and nothing else. They are going public saying that this case is Nova related."

"Wait, wouldn't that affect the election?"

"I have a feeling that's what the mayor wanted once he brought the NCIU in."

"I need to go out with this news."

"No, you can't. We currently have no evidence that a Nova wasn't involved. Also, even if you did right now, it wouldn't make a difference."

"So, I'm supposed to do nothing?"

"Honestly, I don't think you need to. I have a feeling that the murderers won't like having their credit stolen."

"What? You think they are going to retaliate?"

"I'm hoping they go to the press about it."

"That would be stupid of them."

"I think arrogant is the word. If they're the ones that leaked the information to the press then they want to be known and seen. This whole massacre was a big show."

"And if someone were to give that credit away to someone else, they would be furious."

"Well, that's what I'm hoping for."

"What if they go after you guys thinking you're the reason their credit is going to someone else?"

"Don't worry. They most likely know our stand in this whole thing." Richard pulled Mark close to him. Holding Marc in his arms he whispered, "It will be fine. I promise."

"So I have some bad news for you," Alice told Phillip. "You know how you were excited we had a Nova running for the mayoral position?"

"Yes. What about it?"

"Well, the NCIU will be suggesting that a Nova was involved in the massacre that happened."

"Wait. Are you joking?"

Alice looked him in the eyes. "I wanted you to know before the news came out."

He hesitated and finally asked, "Was a Nova actually involved?"

"We currently have no evidence of that."

"So, why are they saying that? Oh, I see. So she won't win."

"Pretty much. It's the whole reason the mayor asked the NCIU to be involved in this."

"Did you try to change their minds?"

"I tried, but they didn't want to listen."

"That's not fair," He responded exhaustingly.

"I told you that it wasn't going to be easy for her to win."

"But at least I thought it was going to be fair."

"There is no such thing as fairness in this world. There is always going to be someone powerful trying to step on the weak."

"But they don't have to."

"It's called fear. Fear that someone might take away their power. But it's a good thing there are people like you fighting against that fear to give everyone the chance that they deserve." Alice cheered Phillip up as she kissed him on the cheeks.

That night Alice was twisting and turning in her sleep, dreaming about that year she went missing. Specifically, the last night she had spent with her teacher.

"Can I ask you a question? How many people have you trained?" a younger Alice asked the bearded old man.

The man looking at the fire they were sitting around. "Only one."

"So, I'm your only student!" She smiled.

"No. I'm not training you. I'm teaching you how to survive."

"Does that mean they're stronger than me?"

"In my life I have brought two monsters to this world. If you stood in front of either of them, you would be nothing but the puddles they step on without even realizing it."

"Are they that strong?"

"Even when I was in my prime, I almost got killed by one of them."

"Who are they?"

"One is on the move. He will soon shake the world."

"What about the other one?"

"The other one is still hiding herself."

"Who's stronger between the two of them?"

"They both have unique qualities about them. One day, they will clash, and on that day the title of strongest will belong to the victor."

"Could you train me to be on their level?"

"No, but you have to figure out your own path. You're doing well now that you have defeated your first Nova. So, you are strong in your own right. I have nothing else to teach you."

"But I'm still not strong enough."

"I can only guide you part of the way. You're the only one who knows what direction you're going," the old man said reassuringly before she woke up.

"Are you okay?" Phillip mumbled half asleep.

"I'm fine. I just remembered something. Go back to sleep."

Chapter 12

The news quickly went wild with the information that a Nova was involved in the massacre and even crazier when news came that Neveah Orcus and her bodyguards were at the top of the list to be questioned. As that news was taking everyone by storm, another story popped up. Marc had released some information that currently the NCIU had no evidence of a Nova involvement and that they were just doing this just to affect the election. He pointed out that it was suspicious that the mayor had brought in the NCIU which conveniently ended up putting his opponent on a suspect list. This caused a bunch of people to support her and volunteer in her campaign. One of those people was Phillip.

It was 6:00AM, and Alice was back at the gym on her day off. She had given herself enough time to heal and couldn't wait to push her limits. She did her regular warm up before a beautiful woman with bright green eyes and a pixie haircut walked in. Saying that everyone was mesmerized by her was an understatement. From afar she was exuding confidence as she approached Alice.

"Hey, Alice, what happened? I haven't seen you in a while."

"Hey, Myra. I needed some time to rest. Sorry I haven't been around," she responded as she hugged Myra.

"You need rest? That's a first." Myra laughed.

"It's been a while since I needed a rest. If I recall, the last time was during our last sparring."

"Jeez, how often do I need to apologize for that?"

Alice looked sad. "Actually, I should be apologizing for not being on par with you."

"I only won because I got lucky that time. Plus, I've never been able to win against you since then."

Alice grabbed Myra's wrist and stared at her. "I know you've been holding back on me. I need you to go all out against me."

Myra smiled at Alice. "Do you know what you're asking?"

"Yes, I do," she responded with certainty.

"Okay, start getting ready. I'll meet you in the sparring area," Myra responded as she walked away from Alice.

When they got there, the gym intercom came on. *"We are sorry but an emergency has just arrived and will require an immediate evacuation of the premises. Please head to the exit door."*

"Great! Why now?" Alice exclaimed at Myra.

Myra started wrapping her hands and getting ready for her spar with Alice. "Why aren't you wrapping your hands?"

"Because we need to leave."

Myra looked at Alice "I don't remember saying you could leave."

"Wait! Did you do this?"

"They do say money talks." Myra smiled.

"You paid them to empty the gym?"

"Well, yeah. Are you telling me that you've never done that before?"

"I'm really in the wrong profession."

"I've been telling you that since I met you."

Alice started wrapping her hands when the club manager arrived. "I just wanted to inform you that the last person left."

Myra placed her hand on his shoulder. "How can the last person have left when you're still here?" she said as she added some pressure on him. The manager, sweating profusely, did all he could to stay up. "I'm sorry, I will be leaving right away." He ran out the door.

"What did you do to him?"

"Just used some of my lawyer skills. What can I say?"

"Looked more like you scared the living hell out of him."

"Look at this face. Could it scare anyone?"

"You can fool other people with that face, not me."

Myra got in position and waited for Alice to finish getting ready. As they started sparring, Alice couldn't help but be amazed at how good Myra was. She felt that Myra's movement was so fluid that it never had an end. As the sparring kept going, Alice got close to hitting Myra a couple of times. She felt hopeful until she noticed that she was always feeling Myra's breath on her fist and always dodging Myra's attacks by microseconds. Myra had gotten Alice's rhythm down and was about to disrupt it.

"The moment you believe that you're not being fooled is the moment that you are," Myra said, before her fist landed on Alice's face, pushing her back. Myra used that moment to throw rapid punches at her.

Alice, unable to dodge the fury of attacks coming at her, tried to move away to no avail. When Alice tried to go right, Myra's fist was already there waiting for her. She needed to step back to regain control—which was just what Myra was waiting for. The moment Alice stepped back, she felt a sharp pain in her stomach from Myra's foot landing a devastating blow, sending her flying off the sparring area.

Alice lay on the floor. "I guess it wasn't luck when you won that first time." She got on her elbows while Myra came toward her without saying a thing. As Myra got close, she tried to kick Alice while she was on the floor, but Alice was able to dodge it.

"What the hell? You won!" Alice yelled.

"Who said it was over?" Myra said as she sped toward Alice and continued her barrage of attacks. Alice picked up a dumbbell and threw it at her. Myra gazed at the dumbbell coming at her and moved sideways as she watched the dumbbell move past her, taking her eyes off Alice for a second. When she turned her gaze back at where Alice was, all she saw was a kick coming at her. She knew she couldn't dodge the kick and jumped back to lessen the hit but tripped and fell down. Alice took the chance to jump on top of Myra, not giving her any room to breathe. Myra took hit after hit from Alice, until she lost her composure and actually got serious. Alice felt a grip on her neck and was pinned down by Myra. She couldn't breathe and the look on Myra's face told her she was going to get killed. Alice tried with all her might to move Myra off her but to no avail. Myra watched as she felt Alice weakening beneath her. Finally, she released her grip. Alice inhaled as much as she could and rolled on the floor coughing.

"What the hell was that!?" Alice tried yelling.

"Sorry, got lost in the moment," Myra replied as she gave Alice a hand to get up.

"You almost killed me!"

"You ask me to get serious because you lost to someone. You're not going to get stronger by being confined to the rules."

"How do you know I lost to someone?"

"Well, it's not that hard to figure out. The news comes out that an assailant beat two detectives investigating the massacre and you don't show up to the gym for a couple days."

"Is it that easy to figure out?"

"When you also add that the first thing you asked, was to fight me seriously, it adds up."

"But what was that about?"

Myra picked up her bottle of water and threw it at Alice. "Drink. It will help." As Alice started drinking some, while Myra continued talking. "Did you know that during our fight you never once went for my eyes or throat?"

"So?"

"So, you have rules. When you're fighting people outside of the sparring area, why do you keep using those rules?"

"Because as an officer, my job is to arrest people, not scar them."

Myra started laughing. "I haven't known you for that long, but I know what you just said was a full-on lie."

"You don't know what you're talking about," Alice responded.

"Do you remember when you told me about the piano wire guy? How you knocked him down?"

"I defended myself."

"Please, you could have easily gone for your gun. You gave him hope so that he would charge at you, and you could release your frustration on him."

"You don't know what you're talking about."

"I just want you to remember that outside, anything can be used as a weapon if you decide to use it."

Alice threw the water bottle back at Myra. "I'll keep that in mind."

"So, how was I compared to the assailant that knocked you out?"

"Should I ask how you know I was knocked out?"

"If you hadn't been knocked out, would you have let the assailant escape?"

Alice smiled. "I guess not."

"So, who's stronger?"

"Hard to say. The assailant was really, strong. One hit almost put me down—but he was stiff and had no technique, which made him easy to read. You lack his strength but make up for it in smooth techniques. Honestly, I would like to see you fight each other."

"Well, next time bring me along."

"Why don't I bring a lawyer with me, too, so I can get sued?"

"Don't worry. I'll only sue the city," Myra replied as they both started laughing. "By the way, are we still on for brunch?"

"Of course, but I will have to leave a bit earlier than planned since I promised I would go support Phillip with his new political career."

"He went into politics? Weirdly enough, I could see that. I mean I don't think he would win, but I can see him trying."

"He's volunteering for one of the candidates."

"Please don't tell me the current mayor."

"No, he's volunteering for Neveah Orcus. I was not aware that you didn't like the mayor that much."

"Actually, I was hoping it was Orcus, since I've always wanted to meet a Nova."

"I guess under normal circumstances it's hard to meet one. I take it you want to come with me."

"That would be nice." Myra smiled.

"Sure, the least I can do since you're paying for brunch." Alice returned the smile.

"Who said I was?"

"I figure since you almost killed me and all."

"Last time I do a favor for someone."

After they were done changing, they made their way to The Blue Sky, their favorite brunch spot.

"So, is a Nova actually involved?" Myra asked.

"You know I can't talk about the case."

"I'm just asking you to confirm what the NCIU said on the news."

"Why are you so interested?"

"I might meet the Nova at the top of their investigation list. She might need a good lawyer." Myra laughed.

Alice took a second before responding. "Honestly we don't have anything saying a Nova was involved."

"Ohhh! A political scandal. How interesting."

"Pretty much, he's trying to win the election."

"That's a dumb move by him. He actually doesn't think people will notice this is a ploy."

"Well, he got elected the first time, so I wouldn't be surprised if people didn't notice," Alice responded as she ate her scrambled eggs.

Myra took a sip of her mimosa. "I guess that's true."

"Enough about my case. How have you been?"

"What can I say? I've been handling smaller cases, but I still have enough time that I can do things like this," Myra replied as she took a bite from her bloody steak.

"Do you ever miss leaving that big law firm?"

"I like having time to myself; makes it easier to plan world domination," Myra replied with a serious face.

"Do I have a high position in that plan of yours?" Alice asked as she laughed.

"Of course not. In my plan, you are my arch-nemesis and our battle will be legendary." Both of them to chuckled.

"So, how are you really doing?"

"I told you, I'm doing fine."

"I know your parents' anniversary is coming up." Alice nudged.

"Why do you need to investigate people that try to be your friend?"

"Because with my job I need to know who I can and cannot trust."

"You didn't need to investigate me to know that you could trust me."

"For all I know, a woman came out of nowhere and befriended me. Also happened to know how to fight and, best of all, is a lawyer."

"What? Seems plausible."

"Stop changing the conversation and tell me how you are doing."

Myra put her elbow on the table and leaned her head on her hand. "I'm going back home for three days to say hi to them and leave them some flowers."

"They must have been amazing parents to have raised a daughter like you."

"Yes, they were. They were strong. They taught me never to back down from my convictions."

"I'm sure they would be proud of the person you turned out to be. I bet you they can't wait for you to visit them," Alice said, trying to reassure Myra.

"I hope so."

"I've been thinking that after I'm done with this case, I could look into your parents' murder."

Myra hesitated before answering. "I appreciate it, but I know the odds. It's been fourteen years since that night. It's hard for you guys finding the guilty party when it's been over six months, let alone fourteen years."

"Sometimes you might just need a fresh pair of eyes. I know you always check with the police to see if they have any new information. So, might as well let me help."

"I feel that you're not going to let it go."

"Nope."

"That would mean leaving the city."

"After this case, that might be a good thing."

"Alright, but what about Richard and Phillip?"

"Richard won't mind helping, plus Phillip will get to go somewhere new."

"Richard won't mind helping," Myra replied in disbelief.

"Even though you two don't get along, he would still help you."

"Can't say I would do the same for him."

"I wish you two would get along better."

"Honestly, how can you even work with him?"

"You get used to it," Alice responded as her phone rang. "Hey, speaking of Mister Handsome, sorry I have to take this," she said as she left the table.

Myra thought about how the mayor was using their plan as a stepping stone to keep power. She thought about killing the mayor, but she knew how childish that would be.

She couldn't help but smile as she pulled out a small red perfume vial. She rubbed some on her wrist and took a sniff. She was doing everything in her power to stop herself from laughing, knowing that the mastermind to Alice's case was sitting across her and she wasn't aware. She thought it was even funnier that she had been wearing her victim's blood all along and Alice couldn't tell. Her cheek started trembling from her trying to hold back her laughter. She decided to think about Mother which helped her control herself.

"Too bad I was the stronger one," Myra whispered to herself.

Alice came back. "So, great news! Richard will be meeting us at the campaign headquarters."

"How is that good news?"

"Because it's funny watching you guys tease each other."

They finished their stuffed French toast and mimosas before heading to the campaign office to meet up with Phillip and Richard.

"What is she doing here? Shouldn't she be freeing a criminal or something?" Richard asked as soon as she saw Myra.

171

"And shouldn't you be arresting an innocent person? Wait! Let me guess. You're here to question the candidate? Because last time I checked, everyone is innocent until proven guilty," Myra replied.

"Are you here to defend her? Now, I'm definitely suspicious of her."

"That's enough." Alice getting in between them. "Now. Let's go meet Phillip, and let's not embarrass ourselves in front of Orcus if we meet her."

"I guess, as the better person, I'll put our feud aside," Myra responded.

"Sure," Richard replied reluctantly.

The three of them headed inside the headquarters, which were massive. Everyone was busy, moving around, making calls. It was obvious that it was more active than usual because of the accusation of the NCIU. All three of them had their reasons for wanting to meet Orcus. Alice wanted to meet the politician that made her husband believe that she would bring change. Richard wanted to meet the woman at the top of the NCIU's list. Myra just wanted to meet a Nova for the first time and see, who truly was the superior being.

As they kept walking, they saw Phillip waving his hand at them from across the room.

"Oh, my God. I can't believe that the whole team is here."

"I wanted to surprise you," Alice replied.

"All right! I have something for all three of you to do," Phillip said.

"Wait, we are supposed to help?" Richard responded.

"Anything I can do to help, Phillip," Myra added.

Richard exhales, "Great. How can I help?"

"I like that both of you just thought that the minute you walked in, you were going to meet Orcus." Alice smiled.

"I figure she would like to welcome her constituents. Especially me."

"Richard, for all we know, she might not even be here today," Myra goaded.

"Honestly, I don't know why Alice even lets a negative person like you tag along."

"Come on, you two. You're embarrassing me in public." Alice exhaled before turning to Phillip. "You want kids? Then handle these two for me, why don't you?"

"Wait! You guys want kids?" Richard excitedly asked.

"We're thinking about it," Phillip answered.

Myra turned to Alice. "That's a lot of work, you know?"

"Well, good thing our kid will have Uncle Richard to boost their ego and Aunty Myra to buy them whatever they want."

"Richard Jr. I like the sound of that." Richard chuckled.

"Hell, no!" Alice responded.

"I don't know, sweetheart. Richard Jr. sounds like a good name."

"Not if you still want to be married to her—and remember I know some great lawyers." Myra jumped in.

"Of course, you do, because soulless demons tend to flock together," Richard whispered before being elbowed by Alice.

"You sure you want a kid when you already have this one here? I heard that children tend to compete with each other," Myra said looking at Richard.

"Let's hope not."

"Okay!" Phillip pulled their attention back to him. "So, Alice and Richard, I'm going to put you two on the calling team. There is a small info session in room 210. You can head there to hear about our policies. Myra, I'm sure I can get you in with the legal team. So, you can follow me."

Myra followed Phillip, leaving Alice and Richard behind. Alice then turned to Richard.

"So, what's the real reason you wanted to come here?" she pried.

"I told you, I'm bored. Marc has to work this weekend. He's getting close to figuring out who sent that information in."

"So, shouldn't you help him?"

"He said he works better alone, that I might distract him. So, he recommended that I spend the day with you."

He dumped him on me, Alice thought to herself. "Oh! Really? There's no other reason? Like maybe wanting to meet the person at the top of the NCIU list?"

"Nope. I'm here for you."

"Sure. Let's just go do our training."

"Yes, ma'am."

After their short training session, Alice and Richard were separated and stationed at phones across the room from each other. After about an hour of calling voters, Alice went on a small walk to stretch her legs. She passed the legal room and saw Myra reading from a pile of papers and talking to her legal team. From where Alice was standing, it looked like Myra was in charge of the team and she was telling them what to do. "How does she do it?" Alice whispered to herself before moving on to check on Richard. As she walked away, she received a text from Myra:

"I'm just that good."

Richard was nowhere to be seen. She walked up to the man that was adjacent to his station.

"I'm sorry, but have you seen the guy that sits over there?"

"He hasn't been at his desk for a while now."

"Thanks." Alice smiled as she walked away. She decided to go to check the kitchen and found Richard eating cereal.

"There you are. Isn't it too late for cereal?"

"It's never too late for free cereal."

"Let me guess. You haven't called anyone, have you?"

"I'll have you know I called one person."

"Wow, one person. That's so amazing." Alice rolled her eyes.

"Well, I've been busy."

"Busy eating."

"No. I've been busy asking around about Orcus."

"Yes, two detectives questioning her team won't seem suspicious at all."

"I figured; might as well know what kind of person she is."

"And what did you learn?"

"Your husband is right. She is an amazing person. Apparently, she is one of those bosses that knows everyone's name and birthday. She apparently knew it was this guy's kid's birthday and sent the kid a gift and gave the dad the day off without him even asking. Also, everyone here seems to trust her completely. Maybe having great memory is part of being a Nova?"

"Well, that's good to hear. Means that we are on the right track."

"I still want to meet her."

"You and Myra."

"Why did you have to bring her up?" Richard whined.

"What's your problem with her?"

"Her smile doesn't seem genuine. It looks like a mask she puts on to hide the way she's actually feeling."

"Maybe she does that because of the way you treat her, or maybe being a woman in a male dominated field, she always has to smile, otherwise she's the woman with the attitude."

"It's more than that. I just feel like I do not know who I'm talking to sometimes."

"Can you try to be nicer to her please?"

"I'll try," Richard replied reluctantly.

"Thank you. Now go back to calling people. I need to check the snacks in here."

"Wait, you're not coming?"

"I called over twenty people. I deserve a break, unlike you."

"The disrespect!" Richard gasped.

Myra had taken control of the room. The first thing Myra did was questioned the person in charge. She went over his plan and quickly brought out the problem with it. Myra did not pull any punches by telling him how his plan was going to do more harm than good. She called all the lawyers to the room. She laid a new plan of attack for them; her plan was to use the fact that the mayor had used his influence to frame Orcus. Everyone looked at Myra and the man in charge. Myra slapped her hand on the table, causing everyone to start moving at her order. Myra turned to the man in charge, "Are you going to stand there or are you going to help?"

The man quickly followed Myra's orders.

It was the look in her eyes. They could tell she was looking down on them, and they could not oppose her. She had also written multiple attack plans against the mayor; some were showing how the only people that benefited during his years in the office have been the rich. After the other lawyers read the plans, they agreed on what was the best course of action and sent the plan to Orcus's personal secretary. Later Orcus's personal secretary came into the room and walked up to Myra.

"Ms. Field, I presume."

"How can I help?" Myra replied.

"Miss Orcus would like to see you in her office."

"I get to meet Ms. Orcus. Intriguing."

Myra followed him to the second floor where a big double door was standing in front of her.

"She is inside," he informed her before going back to his desk.

Myra always wanted to meet a Nova. They were supposed to be the best of the Lessers. She quickly pulled out a hidden necklace, removed the top, and quickly closed it. She needed just one sniff to remove the disgusting smell that she had to endure. She wanted to know how a Nova would smell. Myra opened the door and walked in. She lost her train of thought when she laid eyes on Orcus. Myra was mesmerized by her light pink and blue eyes, and Orcus's natural tan color made her eyes pop even more. When Orcus got up from her desk, Myra noticed the two Nova bodyguards in the room. Both of them wore custom black suits and held a thin sheathed sword in their hands.

"You must be Myra," Orcus said as she walked toward her in royal blue stiletto heels.

Myra inhaled. For the first time, she didn't smell garbage as a human walked toward her.

"You smell nice," Myra accidentally let out.

"Well, I did make sure to put my deodorant on this morning." Orcus chuckled.

"I'm so sorry. I am Myra. It's a pleasure to meet you."

"It's okay. Don't be so stiff."

Myra was having a hard time getting her composure back. There was something strangely soothing about Orcus's voice.

"You wanted to see me?" She asked.

"I wanted to talk about your list of recommendations."

"I gave you the best course of action," Myra replied, finally getting her composure back.

"You gave me a great list, but I'm not going with it."

"What do you mean?"

"If I follow your plan, I could definitely win, but I don't want to win like this. Your plan involves focusing everything on the mayor instead of the people. I'm not running to attack the current Mayor. I'm running to impress the people."

"Do you want to win or not?"

"I think it's funny that you don't think I can win without your plan."

"So, you called me here to tell me that you won't use my plans?"

"No. I called you here to hire you. I like your plan; it just doesn't work with my policies. But you've been here for less than a day and came up with better plans than my team has in the last month."

"I don't think we could work together."

"I disagree. You think I cannot win without your plans, so why not see if that's true or not? If I fail then you were right; if I win then you were wrong," Orcas said with a smile, as she reached out her hand for Myra to shake.

Myra thought. "Deal," she replied, as she shook the Nova's hand. She used enough force to bring an average human to their knees, but Orcus didn't even react to her provocation. On the contrary, she met Myra strength for strength until Orcus finally broke the silence with her laughter.

"I don't know why everyone wants to test their strength on me the moment they meet me."

"I'm so sorry. I didn't realize."

"It's fine. You get used to it. So, since you're going to be working for a Nova, you must have a million question. Go ahead."

"How can you be so positive and nice given your history?"

"My history?"

"What happened to Novaria? What is happening to some Novas even to this day?"

"You mean how most of my people got wiped out. How our country is unlivable, how we got experimented on, or how we get hunted for our eyes? Which one?"

"All of it."

"That's why I'm going into politics. I plan to make sure that never happens again," She said as gloom descended on her face.

"Aren't you scared that you might get attacked?"

"Well, it's a good thing I have my bodyguards."

"Speaking of, what's with the swords?"

"My people originally didn't believe in killing others, but time has changed us. We use a sword so we can see the person's eyes as we kill them so we can never forget."

"Have they used them before?"

"More than I would like."

One of Orcus's bodyguards cleared his throat.

"It seems I have another meeting to attend, but I'm looking forward to proving you wrong." She smiled at Myra while walking her out of her office.

"That would be a first."

As Myra walked out, Neveah closed the doors and replied, "Being the first at everything is what I'm good at."

Chapter 13

Myra walked into her house and hung her keys by the door. She took off her shoes and dropped her workout bag on the floor. Normally, her empty house relaxed her, but not today. Myra felt humiliated that she was being led by Orcus, that she felt like a follower instead of a leader but tried to remove it out of her mind. She closed the blinds to have total privacy and changed into new workout clothes. After changing, she made her way to the basement. She normally worked on her cardio and then did some weights, but today she walked straight to her bench press, added two 45 pounds on each side for a total of 225 and started lifting. After five reps, Myra put the barbell back on the stand. "Not enough!"

She added two more 45 pounds for a total of 315 pounds. She started sweating as she pushed herself, her grip tightened around the bar. Her teeth, grinding on each other, as she pushed herself. "Not enough!"

She added two more 45 pounds for a total of 405. She'd never gone that high before. Her max was always 350 pounds. Today Myra wasn't acting like her usual self. She wasn't thinking about her limit; she just wanted the feeling to go away. She wanted to stop her brain, which kept going back to her interaction with Orcus. She lay down, gripped the bar, and brought it down but this time was different. The weight was too much for her as she tried to lift it back up with her shaky hands. She could feel the cold bar on her chest and there was no one there to help. *When have I ever needed help?* She thought to herself before growling, "Not again!"

She slowly lifted the bar off her chest as she felt the rage twisting her expression into something grotesque, finally putting the bar back on the rack. She got up in the sitting position and held her face in her hand as she panted loudly. She could not help but think of her past, of Mother. Specifically, the first time she felt that weak.

At the Facility, the hunt had kept them on their toes. It would happen once a month. The hunt was one of the many ways that Mother trained them. They would be driven to a forest and given 30 minutes to prepare themselves before being hunted by the Reds—the security team around the Facility. They were called the Reds by the children because during the exercise they would use red paintballs to hunt the kids.

Some of the children stood out from the rest, Luther and Michelle specifically. They were stronger and faster. The other children started to look up to them for leadership, including Myra. Myra would always follow those two during the hunt, until one day she was able to touch the leader of Red team just for a second which was something only Michelle and Luther had done. That day a thought passed her mind. *Why not me?*

During the next hunt, she proposed a game to Luther and Michelle. "Why don't we form teams against the Reds?" Myra asked.

Luther and Michelle looked at each other. "Me versus you should be fun." Luther grinned.

"We could see who the better leader is," Michelle replied.

Those two never realized that Myra wanted to stand at their level. "Why not three teams against each other?"

"Why would we do that?" Michelle questioned.

"Because I want to play against the two of you."

"Why not? It could be fun," Luther replied.

"To make it even more fun, you get to pick your team first." Michelle smiled at Myra.

Myra picked Maxwell who always followed Myra after she helped him deal with killing his turtle. Then she picked Ethan and James because she liked how easy it was to manipulate them. She knew it was not going to be an easy fight. Ten Reds were coming for them. Nine of them had red flags and one had a black flag. They had decided on making each red flag worth 10 points and the black was worth 50 points since it was the hardest one to get.

When the game started, Luther and Michelle went their separate ways with their team. Myra took a moment to decide on their course of action.

"Why are we doing this?" Maxwell asked.

"Because it's more fun this way. It was getting a bit too easy lately." Ethan smiled.

"If it's so easy, why do we keep losing against the Reds' captain?" James added.

"He doesn't count," Ethan quickly refuted.

Myra said, "We are going after the leader."

"Are you crazy? We can't handle him," Maxwell snapped.

"We just need a plan and I happen to have one!" James and Ethan walked up to the leader catching his sight.

"Okay we got this," Ethan said trying to pump himself up.

"If you say so," James replied.

The leader, looking at the two of them, snickered and rushed them. James and Ethan could barely hold out against him as he pummels them to the ground. Out of no where a bunch of leaves start falling from the sky, blinding him. That's when Maxwell jumped down from one of the trees to attack the leader, but the leader punched Maxwell before he could land a hit. Maxwell grabbed his hand, and James and Ethan grabbed his legs. Myra came from behind, going after the flag that was tied to his bicep.

"Not bad," the man said before swinging the kids around like noodles and knocking Myra out.

After the hunt was over, they were taken back to the Facility. That night when everyone was sleeping, Myra went to the classroom. She took one of the chairs and faced it toward the window and sat down. She loved that spot, because she could see the stars a night. As she looked at the night sky, tears started running down her cheeks. She didn't make a sound; she just kept staring at the night.

"It's nice, isn't it?" a voice came from behind her.

Myra jumped up and wiped her tears. She stared at her feet like a scared puppy. "I'm sorry, I wasn't thinking."

The woman moved closer to Myra and looked at the night sky. "Beautiful, isn't it?"

"It's freeing."

"Interesting choice of words." Mother smiled. "Myra, follow me."

Mother took Myra outside the facility. It was her first time outside at night. She sat on a bench in front of the facility and signaled Myra to sit next to her.

"I like looking at the sky from here. It relaxes me."

"So, this is how it feels at night." Myra smiled as the cool breeze hit her face.

"Don't act like you don't have AC in there, but yes, I guess it is different," she said as she put her hand on Myra's head. "So, make sure to savor it."

"Yes, Mother."

The woman kept staring at the stars. "I hear you challenged Luther and Michelle today."

"I thought it would be fun if we made the hunt more interesting."

"How was it losing to those two?"

"It was inevitable."

"Really. So, you'll never try to challenge them again?"

"What's the point? They're much better than us."

"Is that why you went directly to the training room when you got back?"

Myra hesitated for a minute. "Could I ever stand with them?"

"If I said no, would you stop trying?"

Myra thought. "If it means feeling like this forever, then no."

The woman laughed loudly which was a first for Myra. "I wouldn't have it any other way. Those two are special."

"Aren't we all special?"

"Yes, but in many ways, no."

"I don't understand."

"The process is the same, but the seed is different."

"I still don't get it."

"Don't worry about it. I'm not sure if you'll ever stand with those two, but I would love to see it."

Myra looked at the woman. "I promise I won't make you wait too long, Mother."

Chapter 14

Alice walked into their NCIU office. "I finally got access."

Richard, who was sitting at his desk, turned around. "To what?"

"The Witmores' interview."

"You know, we could just go to the cells that they're being kept in."

"I guess you haven't tried, because we are not allowed to speak to them."

"What do you mean we aren't allowed?"

"Only a few people are allowed to see them, and we are not part of the few."

"I knew they were going to push us to the side but not so abruptly."

"I have a feeling that Troy doesn't like you."

"Weird! People usually love me when they meet me."

"Do they?" Alice whispered under her breath.

"Did you say something?"

"Yes. Join me for the interview."

"Actually, I'm working on something right now. Just play it. I'll listen while working on my thing."

Alice took a deep breath. "Sure."

After 40 minutes, Alice leaned back on her seat and rubbed her eyes. "Shit!"

"Are you surprised? The NCIU isn't good at this. They mostly deal with terrorist groups, and they have the power to arrest you just because they deem it. So, how would those people know what questions to ask."

"What a waste of time. Maybe we could talk to Troy and see if he'll give us access to question the Witmore couple?"

"And say what? Hey, Troy, you suck at questioning our only suspects. Let us do it instead."

"Maybe with slightly less jackassery."

"I don't want to be the bearer of bad news, but even if we question them, they wouldn't give us anything we didn't know."

"So, what have you been working on?"

"Glad you asked." Richard smiled and slid a folder at Alice.

She opened it. "Who's this guy?"

With a sad look, Richard answered, "First, he's married."

Alice closed her eyes. "Okay, and the reason you are looking into this guy?"

"You're no fun. I was checking into the marketing firm's history—especially the non-existent one."

"What do you mean?"

"Apparently they were supposed to be one of the investors for the marketing firm but backed out."

Alice looked closer at the folder. "So, what does this Maxwell character have to do with your search?"

"Let's go back a couple of months. Would you gamble on this company?"

"What?"

"Would you put your money on this company?"

"I guess looking at their history, yes. They had a big campaign in the process and many more coming, along with a dedicated team."

"So, why did this guy back out?"

Alice kept reading the folder. "He's an investor. Maybe he saw something we couldn't see."

"Maybe like an impending mass murder?"

"That's a big jump."

"I called his coworkers, and everyone wanted to invest in the marketing firm except for him. He was the sole reason that they did not. So, he is either the most arrogant person that believes he is right above everyone else or he's someone that knew something was going to happen."

"He could be both."

"I also reached out to other investors and ask if the marketing firm was a good investment and all of them said without a doubt. Apparently, they had really strong return, great client list, and the CEO Larry apparently knew who to talk to get the big projects."

"You know investors."

"Okay, Marc knows some investors."

"Sounds about right." Alice stared closely at the photo. "There's something about his eyes."

"I know! I'm in love with them."

"His eyes remind me of the assailant's eyes. I couldn't see his face but could tell he was looking down on us, and I can tell you that this guy is definitely the type to look down on people."

"Well, he's an investor. That's part of the job."

"I guess. So, when do we go visit him?"

"I was thinking now, since Troy seems to be out right now."

"Sounds like a plan. Let's go."

"We're taking my car!"

"Since this is your lead, why not?"

"Yes!" Richard took his car keys and headed to Maxwell's office.

Alice parked the car in front of a big building and got out.

"Wow, talk about big. Guess that's to be expected for being the top investment firm in the country."

Richard got out of the car. "Wasn't I supposed to be driving?"

"I said we would take your car; I didn't say you would be driving."

"Definitely a bully when you were younger."

"I give you a ride and this is how you thank me."

"Yes, you gave me a ride in my own car. Thank you so much."

"You, see? That wasn't that bad." Alice smiled.

They both walked in and headed to the reception desk.

"Hi, we are looking for Global Investment," Alice said with a smile.

"This whole building is Global Investment. Is there someone, in particular, you would like to speak to?"

"Wait! This whole building?!"

"Yes."

"Are you guys hiring?"

Alice pulled out her badge. "Sorry about him. We're here to speak to Maxwell Knight."

"Mr. Knight is on the top floor. Do you have an appointment?"

"We need his help regarding an active case."

"Please give me a second to reach out to him. In the meantime, would you mind waiting?"

"Of course not." Alice smiled.

"You guys could afford to put some candy out to welcome people in next time," Richard said before being pulled away by Alice.

They waited a couple of minutes before finally being approached by the receptionist.

"I apologize for the wait. Mr. Knight is ready for you. Just take the elevator to the top floor and his secretary will show you in."

"Well, let's not keep the welcoming party waiting." Richard smiled as they headed to the elevator.

As they got out of the elevator, a woman stood in the hallway, looking very professional wearing her business outfit, with her hair shoulder length, in heels, while working on her tablet. Upon seeing Richard and Alice, she walked toward them.

"You must be the detectives. I'm Valery, Mr. Knight's secretary. If you wouldn't mind following me, please."

"Guide the way."

As Alice and Richard followed Valery, they took a look at the layout of the place.

"I feel that most of the offices that we visited lately have looked better than the precinct."

"It's called funding," Alice replied.

"At Global, we make sure to take care of our employees as well as our community because that is the only way we can grow together," Valery interjected with a smile.

"Ugh. How can you say those words with a smile?"

"Because they are true."

"Maybe you can have someone else believe that but not me. I have seen firsthand what this company has done. Yeah, it's nice on this side but how many people lost their houses and their savings because of this company," Alice snapped back.

197

"In every investment, there is an equal chance of loss. That's why you should never put in more than you can afford, because otherwise, it's gambling and the only winner is the house." Valery turns to face Alice and Richard. "Behind these doors, Mr. Maxwell is waiting for you. A word of advice: Mr. Maxwell will be the one to lead this company in the future, so please watch what you say."

Those were her last words to the two of them as she went back to her desk.

"Ohh! So scary wouldn't you say?" Richard jabbed at Alice.

"Let's not forget why we are here."

As they walked into the room, Richard instantly focused on Maxwell's chair, especially the leather G embroidered in the cloth.

"Is that a freaking Gen chair?!"

"It's just a chair. Where's Maxwell?"

"That chair costs more than my monthly salary. So, if it's just a chair, then I need a raise."

Maxwell came out of a second door in the room with his tie hanging loosely around his neck and the top of his shirt unbuttoned. "If you like the chair so much, I can get you one."

Alice and Richard turned around, getting caught in Maxwell's violet eyes.   Maxwell walked up to them and reached out for a handshake. "I'm Knight. Maxwell Knight."

"Hi, I'm Detective Richard and this is Detective Alice."

Maxwell walked to his minibar. "Would you care for a drink?"

"No, thank you. We just would like to ask you a few questions," Alice replied.

"Too bad," Maxwell responded as he poured himself a drink. "How may I help you?"

"I'm sure you've heard of the massacre that happened a couple of weeks ago."

Maxwell covered his face with one hand. "I'm sorry, but whenever I think about those poor innocent people, my heart aches for them."

"Do you want to try that again? I think you almost got it. Don't you think so, Richard?"

"I don't know. I think he needed a bit of shaking for my taste."

Maxwell looked at them in anger then after a second, he started laughing. "I guess detectives truly are different, being able to see through me. So, what gave it away?"

"Well, not once did your drink shake. Normally when you hear bad news there's a drawback, especially if they're reacting the way you were. Not once during your acting did it shake. I've seen enough people grieve to know when someone's heart isn't in it," Richard said looking at his drink.

"Why should I grieve for a someone I've never met? I never understood why people even say sorry. What is the point? The dead are just that dead."

"To me, it was your eyes. The emotion in your eyes didn't change. It stayed the same."

"Not much I can do about the eyes, but I'll work on the shaking," Maxwell took a sip of his drink.

"This is not a game! People have been killed."

"People get killed every day."

"You really don't look at people with value."

Maxwell walked to his glass wall and looked down at the street. "When I look at those people walking down there, all I see are machines. They do the same thing every day and not once do they look up. They are always on their phones walking to work, then home, and sometimes they will go out, but the two most important places to them will always be their jobs and their homes. You ask if I see value in them, and the answer is yes, but not on an emotional level. More of a faithful constant. They never change. I know what to expect."

A couple of seconds passed before Richard spoke. "I told you. Investors are just like lawyers. Oh, speaking of, would you be interested in hiring a lawyer? I have someone in mind."

"I didn't realize you came in today to ask for a job." Maxwell laughed.

"We came in today because we noticed that Global was in the process of investing in the marketing firm, but you were the only person who opposed it. Why?"

Maxwell took a sip of his drink. "Every job comes down to knowing the right decision to make. I do a lot of research and spend a lot of hours to figure out what the correct decision is, who are the competition, how profitable are they, do they have a plan for the future, is it a realistic plan, and what will the market be like for them in the future. We had a better investment option—a security company, which we ultimately chose."

"Would you mind telling us why you picked the security company when all your coworkers wanted to go with the marketing firm?"

"There is no such thing as everlasting peace. Do you know there's a finite amount of crime we can handle before people are scared for their lives? The last time everyone was scared for their lives was when the Menean terrorists attacked this country. It's been a decade since then. Looking at the statistics, I notice that crime has been increasing lately and realize it was just a matter of time until things got worse, and if crimes goes up, so will the need for security. The nice thing with crime is that it doesn't just disappear. It takes time and a lot of work to bring it down."

"Sounds a lot like a gut feeling to me."

"Aren't most decisions we make basically gut feelings on some level? Even when we have all the information at our fingertips, our decisions to follow it is nothing but that, a gut feeling."

"Don't I know it," Richard said to himself.

"Where were you on the night of the massacre?" Alice asked.

"I was with my wife at our home that night."

"And your wife would corroborate that?"

"Of course."

"I guess you would know what to expect from her, right? Just like, oh, man, what was the word you used? Oh, yes, a machine, right?" Alice snapped back.

Maxwell's grip tightened around the glass of whiskey as he slung back his drink and put the empty glass on his desk. With a sad smile, he responded, "She's the only one that I never know what to expect from, detectives."

"I have one last question before we leave you. What's inside that necklace of yours?" Richard pointed at his necklace which was visible through his open shirt.

"My wife's blood."

"So, you just carry a vial of your wife's blood around with you?"

"When we got married, we gave each other a small vial of blood so that we could always be close to each other."

"So, if we tested the blood, would it match your wife's?"

Maxwell took the necklace off and handed it to Alice. "Why don't you test it and tell me?"

Richard and Alice looked at each other in shock.

"If you insist."

As Alice and Richard left his office, Maxwell asked. "What's the name of the lawyer you were recommending? I'm getting the sense I might need one."

"Her name is Field. Myra Field," Richard answers as they walked away.

"That was so bad." Alice rolled her eyes.

They left Maxwell's office. As they were walking to Richard's car, he turned to Alice.

"He's involved in this somehow."

"What makes you say that?"

"Gut feeling."

Alice hesitated. "His eyes remind me of the assailant's eyes. The way they both look at you as if you're nothing to them just a toy."

"What do you think is in the vial?"

"His wife's blood, most likely. I doubt it would match any of the victims' blood. Honestly, I just didn't want him to have his way. We have to report this to Troy."

"Yeah, it will be nice to get shut down again." Richard smiled as they both got in his car and drove away.

Maxwell stood in front of his glass wall with his hand in his pocket. He watched as Richard and Alice drove away and smiled.

"Oh, my dear sister, you are having too much fun. I might have to take some of that away from you."

Chapter 15

"So, when will you be coming back?"

"In a week," Myra replied to Alice.

"Neveah must be a great boss that she gave you a week off when you just started working for her."

"She's interesting," Myra replied as she picked up her suitcase. "So, will you be picking me up when I come back?"

"If nothing crazy happens, I'll be your chauffeur. Not many people have a detective as one."

"Here's hoping nothing happens, and thank you for driving me. I know you were busy today," Myra said as she hugged Alice. "Hey, Richard! thank you for helping me carry my suitcase to the car."

"Don't expect that next time, 'cause there won't be one!" Richard yelled from inside the car.

"I'll leave you in Mr. Grumpypants' hands for now," Myra said to Alice as she walked into the airport.

As Alice got in her car, Richard turned to her. "So, the lab just emailed us. The blood matches the wife's."

"Good thing we expected that. So, has the captain set everything up?"

"Yeah, we have some undercover officers following Maxwell."

"That's good. By the way, I can't see what his wife sees in him."

"Who knows? Maybe the violet eyes, or the money, or his handsome look," Richard said lost in thought.

"Which reminds me... how come you didn't jump on him?"

"First of all, I'm a taken man, thank you very much." Richard put his hand on his chest.

"And secondly?" Alice asked.

"The moment I laid my eyes on him, my gut was telling me to get out of there. I'm sure you felt it."

"Why doesn't the wife?" Alice wondered.

"I'm sure she does," Richard said as they drove away.

Myra got on the plane and laid her head back in her first-class seat. She had purchased the seat next to hers as she didn't like having Lessers sit near her when possible. As the plane took off Myra pulled out an empty vial necklace and put it on. "I can't wait to put you inside."

"That's a nice necklace," a man said as he moved from his seat over to hers.

Even though Myra was used to the smell of the Lesser, she had to mentally prepare herself for it, and when that man sat next to her, she was not prepared at all. She was in her own world, thinking of Richard and Alice, how much fun it is to be so close to them and not be seen, especially thinking about how she had the victim's blood hidden around her neck. She didn't even hear the man, but she could smell him and for a split second, she was overcome with rage.

She slowly turned her head to face the man, and all he could see was a monster.

"Where the hell do you get the nerve to move from your seat to mine? If I wanted someone to sit next to me, I wouldn't have bought both these damn seats. Now get the hell away from me before I finish making up my mind." The man stumbled back into his seat, feeling humiliated by the interaction that had just happened. He couldn't look at her but could feel the other passengers looking at him.

A flight attendant walked up to Myra. "Is everything ok?"

Myra smiled at the flight attendant. "Thank you for asking. I think I will be fine in a couple of seconds, but would you happen to have some cleaning wipes? He left his smell behind."

The flight attendant felt that she was looking into the eyes of an angel as she answered Myra, "Give me a second, and we will take care of that right away."

In a soft voice, Myra replied, "Thank you." The flight attendant blushed before leaving to get the wipes.

And that's how it's done, Myra thought as she looked at the man cowering back in his seat.

The flight attendant came back and wiped the seat down for Myra. "You wouldn't believe how often that happens."

Myra gently touched the flight attendant's hand. "Thank you again for caring." Myra knew the effect she had on people as she watched the flight attendant fluster away. Myra poured some hand sanitizer on her hands to clean the filth that she had just touched. During the flight, she kept getting glimpses from the flight attendant and always responded with a kind smile.

As Myra was getting out of the plane, the flight attendant ending up giving Myra her number while shaking her hand as she left the plane.

"Welcome to Inularose, where the fields are roses."

"You could have definitely given me a better last name, but who am I to complain?" she said as she walked away.

Myra had her rituals that she repeated every year, and this year was no exception. Myra stayed at her dead parents' house like she always did when she came back to visit. She went to visit the police department, which had not changed over the years except for the police chief who had more grays than before.

"Hi, Miss Field. Please come into my office." The police chief welcomed her in.

"Do you have any new information regarding my parents?"

"I'm sorry, Miss Field, we don't have any new information. It's been fourteen years. It becomes harder as times goes by to get new information... I don't know if we ever will."

Myra covered her mouth and nose while shedding her tears and with a broken voice said, "This murderer took the people most precious to me, and you are asking me to give up. I'll never give up, because the day I do is the day that they're really gone."

The chief handed her a tissue. "I haven't given up. I promised a young girl that I will never give up on finding her parents' killer, and I never will. But I know the odds and want to make sure you're ready for the worst," The chief said reassuringly.

As Myra was leaving the police department, she could hear the officer talking about her.

"Poor woman. Her parents were murdered when she was only sixteen, and we still haven't found the killer. We probably never will."

Myra went back to her parents' home to rest. The moment she closed the door, she began to smile and started laughing, all the while trying to keep her voice down. After a couple of seconds, she was able to calm down a bit, only to say, "'I told a young girl I would find her parents' killer.'" Myra started laughing hysterically again. "I wonder what your reaction will be when I kill you in the future."

That night Myra had the flight attendant come over to her place.

"So, what do I call you?" Myra asked her.

"Cynthia. What do I call you?" she replied.

"Do you care? You came for one reason, so let's not play games."

Cynthia, upon hearing that tried to kiss Myra, who stopped her.

"Not so quick. My bedroom is on the second floor. Go wait for me there."

"I don't want to wait long."

"There's a lotion near the bed. Put it on."

The following day, Myra brought flowers to her parents' grave. As she stood in front of them, she looked around the graveyard to make sure she was alone.

"All you had to do was tell me what Mother made us for. But no, you had to be loyal to her. I could have made it so painless, but you would not talk. I did learn something important from you two at least. You showed me that having soldiers who are willing to die for you is a must in life." She stooped down. "You taught me how to kill and get away with it. The day I killed both of you, I realized this act of yours only had one ending, and it was your deaths." She put the flowers on the grave and saw a folded piece of paper with a rock on top of it. She opened the paper and read it.

Hello Myra,

Have you been watching the stars? I hope so because I have not had time to.

I love your new haircut. Short hair really works for you.

Good job on g the cult. It's small, but you are still young.

How are your brothers? Can't believe James and Ethan became models.

By the way, could you stop the big performance? The public killing is making me speed some stuff up.

Love Mother

"I haven't looked at the stars in a long time, Mother." Myra put the paper in her pocket and looked at her watch. "A bigger performance is about to start. Hope you enjoy it."

Chapter 16

Back at the mayor's house, there was a fundraiser happening. The mayor had a house big enough to accommodate his donors. Everyone who was entering was welcomed by the waitstaff, with classical music playing in the background as everyone mingled. The mayor also had a small group of six people working on the second floor participating in a telethon. He had learned from past mistakes and made sure to make the room soundproof. The mayor was having his party and reassuring his donors that he would win this election just as he had done in the past. He informed everyone that Ms. Orcus would be a problem of the past just like her people.

In the telethon room, the volunteers were busy calling but also looking forward to the moment they were done so that they could join the party.

A woman in the group got up. "I'm going to close the window. It's getting a bit too chilly." She walked toward the open window and jumped, startled at what she thought she saw. "Oh, my God!"

Another volunteer asked her if she was all right.

After catching her breath. "I thought I saw someone out the window."

Two members of the team walked up to the window and stuck their heads out then closed it. "It must have been the wind. There's nothing outside."

"That was close," James said to himself while hanging beneath the window. "Well, let's keep going." James kept climbing the wall of the house until he reached an empty room. He hooked a malleable piece of silver to his ears and slid his hands across his face connecting the two pieces at his mouth to form a shield. He continued to conceal his face by putting his hoodie on. Finally, the only thing visible was his bright hazel eyes.

"Let the fun begin," he whispered to himself as he walked out of the room. Just as they had expected, the second floor was empty, and everyone was downstairs enjoying the party. He kept walking until he reached the telethon room and went in. As the volunteers saw James, they began questioning him on his identity. James ignored them as he turned to lock the door.

"I'm the entertainment for tonight."

One of the volunteers who was on the phone with a possible donor lost connection. "The phone went down. What the hell is going on?"

James unhooked his mask and removed his hoodie.

"Wait! You're that model. Oh, my God, you scared me," one of the male volunteers gasped.

"You know this man?" the female working next to him responded.

"How do you not know him? James and Ethan: the perfect modeling combo. They always work together. I didn't know this is a masked event. Oh, my God! Is Ethan here?"

James smiled which relieved the room and calmed them down. "Sorry, but he's at another event so you'll have to contend with me."

"To be honest, you're my favorite. Could I get a selfie?"

James snickered as he unzipped his hoodie revealing his perfectly sculpted body. He threw his hoodie by the door.

"Okay, we definitely need to include this in the selfie."

"Tell me something, do you think I could kill you before you call the police?" James smiled.

"What?"

"Do you think I could kill you before you call the cops?"

"In case you didn't realize, we are the telethon team. We are quick callers." The man turned, facing his team. "Right, guys?"

In a split second the man noticed two things. He noticed the look of fear in his co-workers. *Why are they sideways?* was his last thought.

James then snapped the man's neck sideways and punctured his throat with his bare hand. James ran his bloody hand through his hair and exhaled. A big grin appeared on his face as he faced the others. "What are we waiting for?"

After about sixteen minutes, James came out of the room with his mask and hoodie back on. His silver mask had a bloody streak on it and his hoodie was a darker hue. As he leaned back on the door, he heard the mayor downstairs talking to his donors.

As the Mayor was thanking everyone for supporting him and talking about how they were going to win again, he noticed everyone pointing at the second floor above him.

He looked up to see a man wearing a hoodie and a silver mouth covering.

"Who the hell are you? This is a private event," the mayor yelled.

"'Who am I?' you asked. That's a question I've been asking myself for a while now. Can you believe Mother didn't even tell us who we were? Or what our purpose was?" James answered.

"Can someone call security to take out this momma's boy?"

"You might also know me as one of the people that repainted the marketing firm in red. We are Evos, and we only want one thing: to rid this world of this stench." James looked at the mayor. "Sorry for disappointing you, but we aren't Novas."

The mayor and everyone in the room could see his bright hazel eyes. James turned and picked up something from the floor.

"Thank you for letting me repaint your home tonight," James said as he threw something in the air. A person's head landed on the floor in the middle of the room, sending everyone screaming and running.

"Time for this party to end, it seems," James yelled. He pulled out a trigger and pressed it, causing a small explosion outside, which took out the lights in the house as he made his swift escape.

Miles from the mayor's house, a woman fixed her car by the side of the road. She had the hood up when she heard a sound coming out from the bushes. "Is anyone there?!" she yelled.

"Did you wait long?" James came out in front of her.

"No, my god."

"Let's get out of here. I'm still in a great mood and I intend to continue." James smiled at the woman, and both got in the car.

As they were driving away, James looked out the window. "I wonder between my brother and I, who had more fun tonight?"

"But my god, your fun isn't over yet, so let's make sure to have more fun tonight."

Upon hearing that James smiled to himself. "Good thing I have you as my getaway."

At the very moment of James' killing spree, Ethan was at Orcus's headquarters, which were also hosting a telethon that night in the pouring rain. Ethan was on the third floor of a dark parking lot where he was going to sneak into the Headquarters. He already wore his hoodie and silver mask. As he was walking, he heard some footsteps and hid behind a car. A woman came out from the exit of the building, wearing a custom tight suit. Her hair was in a bun, and she was smoking a cigarette with her eyes closed and stopped in her tracks. Ethen had seen her before, she was one of Orcas' bodyguard.

"If I wasn't suspicious of you before, now I definitely am." She turned her eyes towards where Ethan was hiding and revealing her Nova heritage.

Ethan came out from hiding. "I can't believe it. I get to fight and kill a Nova tonight. I always thought that you guys were a bit overrated, with your super strength and all that."

"Should we put it to the test?" The woman smiled.

"At least you seem confident," Ethan said. He sped toward the woman, only to be thrown onto a car as soon as he got close to her.

"Did you just rush me without a plan? Leaving yourself open? Let's try this again, why don't we?" She dusted her blazer off.

Ethan rushed at her with a fury of punches, all of which she easily dodged.

"You're an amateur that only relies on his brute strength," she said, between his missed blows. "You need to take control and know when to attack and defend. Like this." She stomped on the floor and landed a punch on Ethan's ribs, breaking them and causing him to step back. He knew the Novas were strong but never expected it was to this point. "Are all Novas as strong as you?" he asked, holding his side.

"I would say I'm one of the top ten strongest ones."

"That's good to hear. It's going to be even better when I break you. I've been wondering how your blood would smell like. It's about time I found out, wouldn't you say?"

"You're welcome to try," she said as she landed a high kick, which Ethan blocked. "Oh, someone's learning."

Ethan wasn't learning but remembering his training from so long ago. Once Mother threw them out, he and James had only counted on their brute strength, forgetting all of their training, since they didn't need it when fighting most humans.

Ethan was able to finally land a kick, which she blocked but still sent her flying backward. Ethan took that moment to pursue another attack but stopped in his tracks when he saw her glaring at him.

The Nova brushed off the attack and unbuttoned her blazer. She threw it on the ground and rolled her sleeves up. "You didn't continue your attack; that was smart.

You're doing really well. Focus as much as you can, and listen to your instincts."

Ethan realized that he was being treated like a child. Before he could think, she started landing blow, after blow, on him.

"I am a god! Goddammit!" Ethan yelled, all bloody, which caused her to stop and laugh.

"The child believed he was God because he could beat weaker kids than him, until he finally met an adult and realized that this is a bigger game than he thought. Today a god will die, it seems."

Then, a surprised look appeared on her face. "It seems I lost track of time."

Bang! Ethan heard a loud gunshot and could feel the pain on his right shoulder. He turned to see a couple of NCIU agents running toward him, firing their guns. Ethan quickly reacted and jumped off the third floor of the parking lot onto the street in the pouring rain. It was a risky jump, but he knew his body could handle it. He just had to endure the pain. He checked his surroundings to assess the best course of action and that is when his eyes met them for the second time.

Alice and Richard were told to stay behind by Troy and standing right in front of them was the man that had humiliated them.

Ethan didn't have time for this. His body was hurt, and he was tired. He started running, Richard and Alice behind him. Normally, Ethan could outrun them easily, but his legs hurt from the jump. The chase finally ended with Ethan in an alleyway with Richard and Alice. Richard and Alice pulled out their guns. "Put your hands up and do not move!"

"Or what? I have a bullet in my right shoulder, and I have a feeling you want me alive."

"We can always shoot your other shoulder for symmetry," Richard said with rain running down his face.

"True, but I am pretty hurt, so I might die from further blood loss."

"So don't make us shoot you," Alice said as she stepped closer to Ethan.

The second Richard and Alice got close to Ethan, he attacked them. This time, Ethan was slower and weaker than he had been in their previous fight. He still gave Alice and Richard a hard time since they wanted him alive. The fight finally ended when Ethan picked up a piece of glass off the ground to stab Richard with but was shot in the leg by Alice. That only stopped Ethan for a second as he continued to swing the piece of glass downward toward Richard. Alice ended up doing the one thing she didn't want to and shot Ethan through his head, spraying his brain.

"Shit! Shit!" Alice screamed as she rushed to Ethan's lifeless body.

Richard got up. "Fuck. He was our only lead. Let's hope we can get some information about this guy."

"Seems like he got a new mask," Alice said as she removed it.

Richard took a peek. "Oh shit!"

Alice turned to Richard. "You know him?"

"You don't? That is Ethan, the model. I talk about him all the time. I mean it's hard to recognize him with a hole in his head, but that's definitely him."

"You mean your future husband?"

"Not anymore."

"That's good to hear because I prefer Marc."

Richard looked at Ethan's lifeless body, then at Alice. "How do you think his partners are going to react?"

"We'll find out soon enough," she answered as she pulled out her phone and made the call.

A couple of minutes later, the alleyway was full of NCIU officers taking pictures and bagging evidence. Troy was yelling at Richard and Alice on the side for killing their only witness.

"I can't freaking believe this! You couldn't even manage to take him alive? Our only lead?"

Alice stepped up to Troy. "First of all, you shot him first and let him get away. Secondly, it was either letting him kill my partner or him. Don't yell at us like we're children because you can't do your damn job properly!"

Richard followed Alice's lead. "And thirdly, he's not a Nova and from what I hear, neither was the culprit at the mayor's home. So, if you don't mind moving out of our way… by tomorrow this will be our case again. Oh, and when you deliver the body to our coroner's office, would you mind also returning the Witemore's back into our custody? Thank you." Richard smirked as he and Alice walked past Troy.

As they walked away to head to the mayor's house, a thought flashed before Alice, causing her to stop abruptly and run toward Ethan's lifeless body about to be taken away. "Wait! Wait!"

Richard quickly followed behind. "What's going on?"

Alice unzipped the cadaver bag and then Ethan's hoodie, revealing a vial necklace.

Richard said, "Is that what I think it is?"

Alice pulled off the necklace. "I remembered he took some of our blood the last time we went against him and remembered Maxwell's necklace. What are the odds?" She bagged the necklace as evidence.

"I guess I'm not the only great detective."

"Wait. You're a great detective?"

"I'll give you that today."

"I need to tell Myra I won't be able to pick her up tomorrow."

"Thank God."

"I can't wait to tell her I took this guy down!"

Chapter 17

At the same time, in a building across town, a woman was working on multiple monitors facing a crystal waterfall that made the beautiful city light up brightly. Her phone rang. She picked up and listened for a couple of seconds.

"Take care of it." She hung up the phone and went back to work.

A man walked into the room. His blue and red eyes looked like they had a darkness swimming in them.

"I thought I had more time."

"Time's up," the man answered in a deep voice.

"I don't recall saying I was finished," Mother answered as she kept typing.

The man laughed. "You're one of the few that can talk to me like that. Everyone else either grovels at my feet or is killed by me."

"I could see why, when the mighty Darius is standing before them. Me, personally, I don't have time to grovel."

"Just because I respect you doesn't mean I won't kill you. I'll wait for now, but I will personally go when the time comes to pick him up," Darius replied.

"It's not like there's anyone that can stop you."

"I look forward to the day when that's not the case."

"By the way, did you have to kill all my guards?"

"You don't need guards as long as I'm here. Even if the army came, they couldn't do a thing to you."

"Let's not put that to the test. Plus, I'm sure you wouldn't find it that entertaining," she said as she went back to work.

"It never is. They always leave me disappointed." Darius said as he left the room.

Mother stopped working on her computer for a second. "I wish I could have given you some more time."

Chapter 18

James burst into the room screaming at Myra, "Where is he? Where is my brother?!" Maxwell followed right after James trying to understand what was going on.

Myra put her glass down. "You saw the news."

"I want to see his body. I won't believe he's dead until I see his body!"

Myra stared James straight in his eyes. "I don't have the body."

James grabbed her collar and slammed her against the wall. "I saw the news! His body went missing!"

"James. I understand how you're feeling, but you need to calm down." Maxwell tried to reassure James.

Myra, unfazed, stared him down and grabbed both his thumbs and dislocated them, causing him to release his grip, she used the opportunity to tackle him down. "You should never forget this view the next time you try me, because it would be your last."

A tear ran down James's cheek. "I just want to see him."

Maxwell helped James up and fixed his dislocated thumbs by pulling them back into place.

Myra said, "I didn't take the body. I believe that was Mother's doing."

James left the room, furious.

Maxwell, with a confused look, exclaimed, "How could a Lesser beat our brother? It doesn't make sense."

"One of Orcus's bodyguards was there that night. It seems she wore Ethan down enough that Alice was able to kill him."

"How did you not know her bodyguard was going to be there? You work there, for God's sake."

"They never leave her side and there was no reason for them to."

"Could she have known?" Maxwell questioned.

"Not likely. I think she just cares about her workers and wants them to be safe. We have bigger problem: Mother."

"I guess she is coming."

"That's why we need to start preparing ourselves and this facility for her."

"Do you think the Chasers will be able to defeat the Reds?"

"The Reds have been training for much longer, which is why we will be using everyone in the cult against them. The Chasers will be the last line of defense."

"Does that include Elaine?"

"Why wouldn't it?"

"Because she's my wife."

"She's a Lesser. There are many Elaines in the world."

"Not to me."

Myra looked sadly at Maxwell. "Do you want her to live the rest of her life having to wear the cream just to make your life more comfortable? Is that the life you want for her? At least letting her die for you will give her life meaning."

Maxwell snickered. "I see it now."

"See what?"

"You can act sad, but your eyes say otherwise."

"My eyes?"

"Someone recently told me that my eyes weren't displaying sadness. I'm looking into the same eyes right now."

"Wish I knew that before," Myra said, smiling to herself.

"Can we trust you?"

"Shouldn't I be the one asking you that?"

"You know I care about our brothers and sisters."

"I know you do, but hasn't your priority shifted?"

"I still want to find Mother. That hasn't changed."

Myra stared into space for a second before looking at Maxwell. "How was the doctor's?"

Maxwell's expression changed. "Excuse me?"

"What was the result?"

Maxwell clenched his hand into a fist. "I should have known. I can't even have some privacy!"

"We were born in a lab; we've never had privacy."

Maxwell took control of his emotions and let the words out. "I can't have kids."

"Does she know?"

"I haven't told her yet."

"You sure it's not Elaine?"

"You think I wouldn't make sure I had the correct information?"

"I see. I was worried about that."

"Me and Elaine not being able to have a kid is of no concern to you."

"But it is. Don't you see what that means?"

"That I don't have a future?"

"That we don't have a future. I'm sure you're not the only one infertile. Mother wouldn't have missed that.

What's the point of creating superhumans when we can't reproduce?"

"But she told us that we are the next evolutionary step!"

Myra took a couple of steps back and sat on the side of her desk without saying a word.

"Say something! Was our existence a lie?!"

Myra closed her eyes for a second and took a deep breath. "You can still leave. You could go to your cabin with Elaine and live peacefully there. You don't have to kill. You could grow old together."

"Just to have you come and kill us?"

"You are my brother. We were both born in the same lab. I would never kill you."

"I find that hard to believe."

"I would kick your ass if I felt there was a need to, not kill you or James. Otherwise, I would be the only one left with this addiction."

For the first time in a long time, Maxwell relaxed around Myra and started laughing. "I have the same addiction, so I don't think that I could live in the cabin peacefully. Plus, I have a feeling the cops will arrest me soon, so staying on a lawyers' good side right now might be beneficial."

Myra smiled. "I guess you're lucky that I'm a great lawyer. So, do you think the cops will be on you soon?"

"If they got Ethan's necklace, then yes."

"Let's work with the belief that they probably have the necklace. You should have your company's lawyers prepped by informing them that the police have been following you and your wife for some time now, and you don't feel safe even going out anymore. Show them this picture and that should take care of your problem. It will also show that the police were investigating a case that was under the NCIU, showing that this might be personal on some level," Myra said as she pulled out a file from her desk, revealing pictures of the officer following Maxwell and Elaine.

"You really are good!" Maxwell took the photographs from her.

"Now that I've helped you, can you go talk to James and make sure that he doesn't do anything too crazy? If he needs to kill a Lesser to blow some steam off, can you take care of it for him?"

"So, you do care." Maxwell smiled.

"Of course, I care, but I need to always be able to take a step back to see the whole picture. Letting my emotions get the best of me will cause more of my brothers to die."

As Maxwell was about to leave the room, he stopped. "Sorry for putting everything on you."

Myra tilted her head backward and exhaled as Maxwell left. She took a sip of her drink and poured the rest on the floor. "It's hard to take a step back," she said as she crushed the glass in her hand, letting her blood drip and mix with the alcohol.

Maxwell found James in his personal fitness room, punching the wall.

"Try not to break the facility. It costs a lot of money to fix these room."

"This place means nothing without my brother. He's dead!" James yelled as he cracked the wall with his bloody hands. "It's her fault. You and her both don't care about us. You guys weren't-"

"That's enough!" Maxwell cut him off. "You know how many Lessers we have killed. They finally kill one of us and you are whining about it."

"Our lives are worth more than theirs. It's our right, because we are stronger!" James said as spit flew out of his mouth.

"And Ethan lost because he was weaker. My own brother lost to a human! How do you think that makes me feel?"

"Shut up!" James screamed throwing his fist at Maxwell, which Maxwell easily stopped, grabbing his brother's bloody fist. "Do you think Ethan would be happy with the way you are acting right now? He could have just gotten arrested, but he fought till they killed him. Do you know why?"

James dropped his fist, and more tears came down his cheeks. "So that we could continue."

Maxwell pulled James into his arms. "Yes, and we are close to the finish line."

"I don't know what to do with these feelings."

"Hold them until we meet Mother again."

James pulled back and growled. "Mother."

"Do you want to go on a hunt?"

"I want to be alone and heal my hands."

"Don't do anything crazy." Maxwell patted his brother's shoulder as he left James and went home.

The moment Maxwell got home; he was welcomed by Elaine.

"How did it go?" she asked.

"James didn't handle it well. Myra tried to keep everything to herself."

"I'm sorry I couldn't be there for you today."

"You're being followed. It might be good to stay away from the facility from now on. Why don't we go to the cabin and stay there for a couple of days?"

"Don't you have work tomorrow?"

"So? I will take a sick day. I just want it to be just the two of us for a couple of days."

"I'm sorry, but I can't do that."

"Why not?"

"There's been some chatter since Ethan got killed. People are suspicious that you might not be gods."

"That's to be expected."

"If I can reassure everyone that the only reason Ethan got killed was that he was surrounded by a Nova and multiple cops, maybe it can stop the chatter."

"Don't worry. Just leave everything to Myra. She can take care of it. I just want you to be safe, especially now."

"I know you'll never let anything happen to me," Elaine said as she embraced her husband.

Maxwell peeled her off him. "I got the result from the doctor. It's not possible, because of me. I'm taking so much away from you."

Elaine remembered that look. She had seen it the night she almost died. She said, "You have given me more than I could ever hope for. You made me stronger, you gave me the courage to trust again and to me, that is worth the world. You are the God that cried for me."

Maxwell took a deep breath and closed his eyes, trying to hold back tears, tucking his lips in his mouth, and pushing his emotions down. He finally exhaled as a tear rolled down his cheek. "I've always wondered if I could feel. I kill and enjoy it, but I was created to kill. I never felt any other emotion, only rage and the joy I get from killing. When you came into my life, you woke emotions I never knew I had. To me, you are my goddess. You gave me meaning beyond that I was created for. You make me believe I can beat this addiction—but now I'm scared that I might lose you in all this."

"You'll never lose me, because you'll always be there for me."

Chapter 19

The NCIU had decided to step away from the case.

Back at their desks at the precinct, Alice and Richard both were trying to wrap their heads around losing Ethan's body.

"I still can't believe we lost the Witmores and Ethan's body." Alice groaned, flipping through the case file.

"Technically, those two things happened under the NCIU, so we didn't lose anyone," Richard corrected her as he was enveloped in the case's documents.

"It doesn't matter under whose watch! Two of our suspects escaped and the only other lead we had got stolen," Alice responded frustratingly.

"We still have the necklace."

"What good is that when we can't question Maxwell because of his lawyers?"

Richard stopped and rolled his chair to Alice's side. "Can I see those pictures of our officer again?"

"Why?" she asked as she passed the pictures to Richard. Richard went through all the photos and stopped at one. He brought it closer to his face. His eyes bulged as he jumped out of his chair. "Caffeine. Now. We must have coffee. Let's go." Richard practically dragged Alice and the files to their favorite cafe.

As he walked in, he told a confused Alice to find a table as he placed the order. "Okay, why drag me here?" Alice asked as Richard sat down with the coffee.

"Who took the pictures?"

"Maxwell probably hired some to take them."

"But how did he know when to hire someone? Look at this picture." Richard slid the photo back to Alice.

"It's our officers in their car."

"That's the first day they started tailing him and his wife. So how could he have hired someone on the first day that he was being tailed?" Richard grinned with confidence.

"Because he knew we were coming."

"Remember our first lead and the hunch we had of a mole? We need to find him as soon as possible before he makes this worse. He's probably the one that stole the body."

"Unfortunately, finding the mole is the easy part. Making him talk will be the hard part."

"You have something?"

"So, we know he leaked the information out to the press. We know he told the Knights that we were tailing them."

Richard smirked. "That's a lot of lead."

"So, did Marc ever find out who leaked the information to the press?"

"All he could gather is that it was a man that called the information in."

"Okay. That eliminates about thirty-six percent of the officers."

"When we asked the captain to have some officers follow the Knights, he kept it low profile," Richard added.

"So, it would have to be one of the undercover detectives."

"Unless they talked to other officers about it."

"I'm sure the captain would have told them to keep quiet in fear of it reaching Troy's ears." Alice rebutted.

"One of these detectives should have been working on the day we went to the cleaning lady's apartment."

Alice looked at the photos of the men. "I remember seeing Duane, Dale, and Jacob that day."

"Out of those three, who could be the mole?"

"It's most likely Jacob," Alice replied.

"Why him?"

"You really need to get to know your co-workers better."

"I know you."

Alice took a sip of her coffee and made a disgusted face. "I believe this caramel is yours. I think I just lost some brain cells."

"Don't insult the coffee."

"Is that what you want to call it?" Alice replied as she took a sip of her coffee. "That's how it's supposed to be."

"Okay, so, how do we prove it?" Richard asked.

"Let's have Marc follow Jacob for a couple of-"

"No" Richard cut Alice.

"We can't follow him or have another officer follow him. It needs to be an outsider, someone they never meet before. Plus, as a journalist, he knows how to follow people and get information safely."

"I said no."

Alice exhaled. "Sorry for asking. I just want to solve this case as quickly as possible."

"I can't help but feel someone is using us to enjoy themselves."

"What do you mean?" Alice asked.

"They know who we are. They made sure to put us back in charge of the case by attacking the mayor's house."

"Do you think it's Maxwell playing us?"

"Maybe. We know that there were four fingerprints at the 'advertisement massacre'. If we can get Maxwell's fingerprints, it would be a slam dunk. Too bad he wiped the necklace before we got to his office."

"We also killed one of the culprits, so we're left with two men and one woman. On top of that we are still having a hard time reaching James," Alice replied.

"Never expected I would be looking for James this way."

"Neither did I."

"So, who are the other two? And why wasn't the woman active during the recent attack?"

"Since there's only two candidates running, they only needed two members for the attack," Alice answered.

"How convenient is it that Orcus had her guard on duty that night?"

"I thought we agreed that she had nothing to do with it."

"It's simply weird that one of her personal guards wasn't with her that night. Usually, they never leave her side."

"I see your point, but on the night of the massacre, she was on TV talking about her policies, which she made sure to bring up during the NCIU questioning."

"I guess," Richard replied.

"Let's work on Jacob first. Maybe everything else will fall into place," Alice said reassuringly.

"All right. How do we prove he's a mole?"

Alice took a second to think. "He was working on the night we got assaulted. We left our file on the table. I bet if we go back and check the security camera, we'll see him going through our files."

"That's not proof that he's the culprit."

"Yeah, but if we can use that to get his phone records, it should lead us to something."

"So, we're in the hoping game now?"

"Do you have a better idea?"

Richard sighed. "That's if we can get a warrant without anyone else finding out."

The following day at the precinct, Alice was going over everything in the file for the hundredth time when she stopped. "Wait a second!" She turns to Richards. "Can you pass me the mayor's file and Orcus's?"

"Did you figure something out?"

"I need to make sure."

Alice sat down and studied the files intensely for a few minutes. "I got it!" she yelled in excitement.

"We got it! What did we get?" Richard slid his chair closer to hers.

"We couldn't see it before, because we assumed the cleaning lady was their connection to the inside, but that was just a front to throw us off."

"So, when we got attacked in the alleyway, it was to reinforce that idea?"

"I noticed something the first time but paid it no mind. However, when you consider the other attack, a pattern seems to form. Look here: this guy was hired by the marketing firm six months prior to the attack. The mayor's private security team hired someone new six months ago and, with Orcus, this woman right here was hired six months ago, too. This time frame can't be a coincidence."

"At the mayor's home, they had an inside man way before we were even on the case." Richard's eyes widened with excitement.

Alice paused. "How did they know to send someone into the mayor's and Orcus' headquarters?"

"That was probably the easiest part. They knew Orcus was running for the mayoral office and knew that if a big massacre happened that seemed to point to a Nova, the mayor would most likely try to blame her to keep his job."

Alice looked around to see if Jacob was nearby. "I think now is a good time to go check on our new suspects. And let's make sure we take our files this time."

"You get the car while I get the address and files."

A long drive led them to one of the suspect's houses. Alice parked the car and they started walking toward his house. As they got closer, they noticed smoke coming from the house and the suspect escaping from behind it.

"Check the house!" Alice yelled at Richard as she ran after the escaping man.

The second Richard opened the door, he could feel the heat on his body. He saw the fire spreading but he knew he still had some time. He needed to find something to help their case. Richard quickly rummaged through the suspect's mail.

"Crap, crap, crap!" he yelled as he kept coming up empty. The growing flames made the situation worse as he couldn't concentrate. Richard started looking around.

"Okay, where would I hide my dirty laundry?" He stopped for a second and started stomping on the wooden floor looking for a secret area, quickly moving around.

"Shit! nothing!" He headed to the second floor, leaving his escape sealed behind him with the burning flame. Richard frantically looked around the bathroom, the bedroom, and finally the closet where he saw the same gold sculpture in the shape of an eye that was at the Witmores' house. He remembered there was a secret compartment at the bottom of the sculpture. Richard opened the compartment of the sculpture, finding a small notebook, and grabbed it.

He couldn't go down the stairs anymore. His only exit was the window. Sweating and coughing, Richard struggled to open the window but finally succeeded.

"Tuck and roll," Richard repeated to himself before finally taking the jump off the second floor, screaming in pain as he landed.

A couple of blocks away, Alice caught up to the suspect. He was fast, but Alice knew she was faster.

In normal circumstances, the man would stand his ground, but he knew from his companions he couldn't beat Alice. His only hope was to escape.

Alice didn't want to use her gun, because they were in a crowded street, and she didn't want to kill him. She was confident enough in her speed that she knew it was a matter of time until she caught him. As she got closer to him, she heard a gunshot and saw the suspect's brains fly out of his head. In a matter of a heartbeat, she glanced around and hid behind a nearby car. She remembered the direction of the bullet and tried to peek but heard another gunshot. She felt the bullet pass by her and hid. She knew she wasn't that lucky. It was a warning shot.

"Stay down! Find cover"! she yelled to the pedestrians. "Shooting occurring! Possible sniper! Backup needed ASAP! Get your asses down here now! And bring an ambulance, too!" she barked into her phone.

A minute passed before she was able to deem it safe enough to quickly run to the dead body. She looked at the wall and saw the bullet hole. She did some basic calculations and aligned the building where the shooter might have come from. This was done by a professional. The suspect was in a crowded street, running and still got his head shot. Alice called Richard and got no answer. She also radioed Richard's location to make sure he was safe.

Far away from the crime scene, a man and woman drove away in their car. The man made a call.

"It's done."

"We will be waiting for your next order." The man hung up.

"I don't see why Mother doesn't let us just kill them," the woman said as she lit up her cigarette.

"Because she's her favorite," the man answered.

"We'll take care of that soon enough," the woman replied as she kept smoking.

Chapter 20

As soon as backup arrived, Alice dashed to Richard's location. At the burning house, she saw multiple firemen fighting the fire and an ambulance leaving the scene. Alice ran to one of the firemen.

"Was anyone inside?" Alice questioned.

"Ma'am, please move aside. This is an emergency."

Alice showed her badge. "Was there anyone inside?"

"No, there was one man outside who was hurt, but he just got taken away by the ambulance."

"So, he's alive," Alice said with relief.

"But he does seem to have a broken leg."

"He'll heal fast. How long until you guys are done here?"

"Maybe an hour."

"Can you do it faster?"

"If you let me go do my job, we might finish a bit quicker."

Alice let the man pass and she called Marc to inform him that Richard was in the hospital. She made sure to send some officers to some of the buildings where the shots might have come from. Maybe they could get the security video for her to review later.

After the firemen were finished, Alice walked over the wet, charred floor looking for any hint of a clue, but any evidence that might have been left behind was burned. When she was done with the crime scene, she headed to the hospital to check on Richard.

The minute Alice stepped into the room she was welcomed by Marc and Richard.

"Why is it that this case keeps putting you in the hospital?" Marc asked.

Alice looked at Richard's leg cast. "Let's hope this is the last time."

"You best believe it's the last time. My insurance can't afford any more visits," Richard replied.

"This is not funny!" Marc replied angrily.

Richard held Marc's hand. "Bad things sometimes happen. That's life, and you can't control it. What I can control is what we are having tonight for dinner." Richard smiled at Marc.

Marc smiled back and kissed Richard. "Actually, I can. We are having salmon tonight."

"I guess we're having salmon tonight. Could you get me some coffee, please? I need to talk to Alice."

"Sure, but I'm not getting you any caramel."

"Of course not. I promised, remember?"

Marc left Alice and Richard alone in the room.

"Is it as bad as it looks?" Alice asked.

"Just broken. I remember when I could do a jump like that without breaking a sweat." Richard said as he got off his bed.

"Don't think about it. You'll be back on your feet in no time."

"I'm already on my feet. Can't you see that?"

"Without the crutches."

"You're so hard to please. Maybe that might do the trick," Richard said as he pointed toward the table by the bed.

Alice picked up the notebook. "What's this?"

"I found it in the house. You didn't think I would just come out empty handed, did you?"

Alice gripped the book. "Of course not."

"Don't get too excited. I went through it. There are no names."

"Still, it's something we didn't have before."

"On the plus side, it is a cult like we suspected. Even better… they follow four gods and one of them is a woman."

"That fits with our first assumption."

"I keep telling people we are amazing at our job, and they always seem skeptical. I can't wait to tell the chief."

"We will need to keep this under wraps, considering the mole."

"It's not like I was going to scream it to everyone at the precinct." Richard pouted.

"Anything else?" Alice askes while flipping through the pages.

"Apparently, there's some doubt building up in the group because of Ethan's death."

Alice's phone rang. "What is it?" she answered.

Richard could see a look of frustration on her face as she hung up her phone. "Bad news, I take it?"

"I sent some officers to the other two suspects' houses. Seems their houses were also burned down."

"On the plus side, we have enough evidence to get a warrant to track their cell phone."

"And if we can show that a call came from Jacob's phone, that would also be enough proof that he's the mole!"

Richard hopped to Alice's side and high fived her. After Marc returned with the coffee, Richard split up with Marc at the hospital and headed to the precinct with Alice.

They walked into the chief's office and closed the door behind them.

"Please tell me you have something this time," the chief said.

"Do you need to ask when I'm on the case?" Richard answered smugly.

"Should you be talking with that leg of yours?" the chief said.

"Please. No broken leg can stop me."

"Sorry Chief. Next time I'll remember to leave him behind," Alice commented. "We actually have quite a lot," she continues.

"Alright, I'm listening."

"We are currently dealing with a cult."

"A cult?"

"Led by four people, which I'm 90% sure that Maxwell is one of."

"We had agents tailing him and never saw anything suspicious," the chief added.

"That's because he knew we were coming," Richard jumped in.

"What do you mean he knew?" the chief asked with a stern look.

"We believe that someone inside tipped him off."

"Do you know what you're saying?"

Alice pushed. "Do you think we would suggest it if we weren't sure?"

"Then what's your evidence?"

"There was the fact that the day we went to the cleaning lady's house, we got assaulted as though they knew we were coming," Richard said, leaning on his crutches.

"That's not evidence."

Alice took out the pictures that Maxwell had taken of the officers tailing him and his wife.

"Look at this photo."

The chief took the photo. "Those are our officers."

"That's the first day he was being tailed. How did he know we were tailing him?" Alice continued

"Maybe he saw them?"

"So, on the first day, Maxwell saw our officers and went to hire someone to take pictures of them. All on the same day," Richard said sarcastically.

The chief looked at them. "Okay, you might have a point. Who do you think it is?"

"We think it's Jacob."

The chief turned to Alice. "Why Jacob?"

"You told us you kept it low-profile and only informed the officers in the pictures."

"So, it could be any one of them," the chief added.

"No, because out of all of them, he's the most likely to be coerced into joining a cult. Especially after what happened to him in the past," Alice pushed.

The chief thought about it for a couple of seconds. "Okay. How do we prove it?"

"When we got to one of our suspects' houses today, he had set fire to it and was running away like he was informed that we were coming," Richard jumped back in the conversation. "Then, we found out our other two suspects' houses had also been burned down. If we can get the phone record of our three suspects, we should be able to find out who called them before we got there."

"I'm guessing you want to keep this quiet for now. I know someone who might be able to help."

"Thank you, sir."

"Yeah, thank you, Chief. Now, about my paid time off for the broken leg, I think one month is more than enough."

"You mean your desk duty of two weeks."

"Two weeks! What am I, an animal!?"

Alice rubbed her forehead, feeling a migraine coming.

"I know for a fact that it will take two weeks at most to heal." The chief replied.

"It's not just my leg that needs to be healed, so does my mental health."

"From what?!"

"From this traumatic experience."

"Well, I'm sorry to tell you you're in the wrong field!"

Alice tries to drag Richard out before he made the situation even worse but couldn't keep his mouth closed.

"You'll hear from my lawyer."

"I don't pay you enough for a lawyer!" The chief yelled at Richard.

Finally, they were out of his office and back at their desk. Alice turned to Richard.

"I can't help but remember Marc telling me it was going to be a week for you to get back on your leg because of Teltius technology."

"Yeah, what's your point?"

"You do know when the cast comes off the chief will just put you back on the street with me."

"Son of a gun."

"Nice try though. So, what's the real reason you want to be on desk duty?"

"We've gone against these monsters twice and both times I've only gotten in the way. Now that I have a broken leg, I will only hold you back. Are you going to be fine without me?"

"You'll be here with me, plus you can keep an eye on our good friend here. May get to know him a bit more." Alice winks at Richard.

Richard lay back at his desk. "Sounds exhausting. I'm guessing we aren't going to the other houses?"

"I'll wait to get the fireman's report. Which will give me time to finish today's report."

"Can you do mine also?" Richard asked with his puppy eyes.

"Weird. Your hands don't seem to be broken."

"You and the chief should learn to be nicer to people in pain."

Alice pulled out her phone and started texting. "Sure, what you said."

"Texting Phillip, I take it."

Alice put her phone in her pocket. "Why? Would you like to invite us over for dinner tonight?"

"No, it's just that I haven't received a text from him asking how am I doing."

"Give it a minute." As Alice said that, Richard's phone started buzzing. "Told you."

Richards read it. "Awww, he's so good to us."

Alice shakes her head with a smile. "Stop saying that."

"He would have done my report for me," Richard said under his breath as he started working on his report.

Later, Alice drove Richard home, where Marc was waiting to take him inside.

"Thank you so much for bringing him home. I owe you one," Said Marc.

"You don't owe me anything. You're taking him off my hands tonight. That's thanks enough," Alice answered as she drove away.

Alice pulled into her garage after midnight, exhausted. She stayed in the car for a couple of seconds to recoup what little energy she could before taking the files and notebook out of the car.

The house was pitch dark since Phillip was already asleep. Alice navigated in the darkness and put the files and notebook on the table. She headed to the kitchen to get a glass of water. She did not turn the kitchen light on, not wanting to wake up Phillip.

As she tilted her head back to drink the water, her vision caught a glimpse of silver behind her before her world went dark.

Cold. Cold and wet. That's all Alice felt as she woke up. She felt restraints against her wrists and tape over her mouth. She saw Phillip in front of her, also restrained and gagged, and realized they were in their bedroom.

Both tried to communicate to each other to no avail.

Finally, the bedroom door opened. A man with a silver mask and bright hazel eyes made his way into the room. She saw the notebook that had rested on her table.

"You shouldn't have this," the man said.

Alice tried to mumble through the gag.

"Let me take that off for you." He ripped off Alice's tape. "I usually don't do the torture thing so be patient. Also, you should know not to scream. You know what I can do."

"What do you want?" Alice asked.

"We'll get to that later. For now, your eyes tell me that you know who I am. So, tell me. Who am I?"

"James."

The man pulled off his mask to reveal his face. "How did you know?"

"Your eye color and your relation to Ethan."

"I figured it was a matter of time anyway," the man said as he read the notebook. "Have you read it yet?"

"The important parts, like your stupid little cult. Don't you feel embarrassed?" Alice said as she kept looking at Phillip to reassure him that everything was going to be alright.

"We were born to rule over you Lessers."

"Lessers are supposed to be everyone but you guys, I take it."

"That is correct."

"So, what does that make Ethan, then?"

James wrapped his fingers around her throat and lifted her up with the chair, watching as she gasped for air. Phillip tried to scream and struggled, unsuccessfully to stop him. After a couple of seconds, James put her down and released her throat.

"Sorry about that. I seem to lose it when it comes to my brother."

Alice, still coughing, could feel the remnant of his hand around her throat.

"Does Maxwell know you're here?" Alice powered through the pain to ask that question.

James put the tape back on Alice's mouth. "I always thought that the worst thing you could do to someone is kill them, but when you killed my brother, you taught me that I was wrong. You asked me before why I was here+" James turns to Phillip. "To bring you to my hell."

Chapter 21

James walked out of the room with bloody hands. He turned the stove on to burn the notebook. Then he went back to the living room, where he picked up Alice's cellphone and scrolled through her contact list until he found Richard's number. The phone rang a couple of times.

"Alice, do you know what time it is?"

"That's a rude way to answer your partner."

"Who are you?"

"Shouldn't you be asking what happened to her instead?"

"Where's Alice!? What have you done to her?!"

"Instead of yelling, why don't you come and check on her?" James said. He hung up the phone and left as the fire in the kitchen spread.

"Don't be too late!" James snickered as he walked out the door.

Richard quickly called officers to go to Alice's house, then Marc drove him to Alice's house, disregarding the speed limit and all traffic lights.

The house was engulfed in flames. Richard tried his best to run toward the burning house, screaming Alice's name, only to be stopped by the officers on duty and Marc.

"Where are they?!" Richard shouted.

The officer couldn't look Richard in the eyes but pointed toward the ambulance. Even with a broken leg, he tried his best to run. Finally, he saw her, covered with a sheet except for her head.

Richard hugged her. "Oh my God! You're alive!" Richard pulled back to look at her and hugged her again. "I thought I lost you!"

Marc looked around, saw Alice was alone, and covered his face, holding back his tears as he realized what had happened.

Richard couldn't think of anything else but his partner. "How are you doing?!"

For the first time, Alice opened her mouth. "It seems that I'll need a new place to stay." Her eyes without emotion as she said those words, trying to keep reality at bay.

"Don't you even think about that. You and Phillip are welcome to stay with us." Upon saying those words Marc started crying as he was unable to hold back his tears anymore. Alice's face didn't change, it stayed dead, but her hand started shaking and she brought it closer to her face.

"Weird I can't seem to stop the shaking."

"It'll go away after some time. Don't worry about it. Do you know which hospital Phillip is at so we can go see him?"

Alice's hand started shaking even more. "Why would he be in a hospital? He's just working late tonight. Good thing he wasn't home." As those words left her mouth tears started flowing down her cheeks as her face still remained dead. "Can I borrow your phone? I need to call Phillip and tell him I'm all right."

"Of course," Richard said as he went through his pocket to get his phone. As he was about to pull out his phone, Marc stopped him. "What are you doing?" he asked Marc.

Marc shook his head.
Richard didn't let that stop him and pushed Marc's hand away. "I don't know what's gotten into you, but she needs us right now!"

Marc couldn't muster up the strength to tell him.

"Let me dial the number for you." Richard handed the phone to her.

Alice, with her trembling hand, put the phone to her ears. With each ring that passed, her hand started shaking even faster. When she got Phillip's voicemail, she dropped the phone on the floor. She turned to Richard's and this time it wasn't just tears that were running down her face but also sadness. Richard quickly realized what that meant.

"No, no, no, he's probably so busy at work that he can't answer," he said as he turned to Marc looking for validation and finally was able to see the tears on Marc's face. Richard couldn't hold in all the evidence that he kept at bay the moment he arrived on the scene: the officer telling him that only Alice had survived, Phillip's car being in the driveway. It came rushing in like the tears rushing down his cheek. Richard held on to Alice as she let out one loud scream.

Chapter 22

In the morning at Richard's apartment, one of his cats sat meowing in front of the guest bedroom. Finally, Richard came and picked her up.

"Sorry, little one. She still needs some time. Why don't we get you some food?" he said, carrying the cat to the feeding station where the other two were already eating. The second Richard put her down, she ran toward the door and started meowing all over again.

Marc came out of their bedroom.

"Nema still won't leave her alone?"

"No, it's been like that since we brought Alice home five days ago. They're both so stubborn. Alice won't leave the room and Nema hasn't moved," Richard answered, depressed.

"It's not your fault. So don't handle everything on your own," Marc said as he held Richard's hand.

"It is!" Richard yelled, pulling his hand away from Marc's. He gazed at Alice's door and put his hand on the counter. Richard started breathing deeply to calm himself down. He didn't want to yell while Alice was in the house. He turned his head toward Marc to see the look of helplessness on his face.

"I'm sorry," Richard said as he tried to hold on to Marc's hand.

"I know this is hard for you right now. It's hard for me, too, and even more so for her. So, don't turn this into something about you."

Richard took a second before replying, trying to control his anger. "Do you know why James killed Phillip? Because Alice killed Ethan. And do you know why Alice killed Ethan? To save my life! I couldn't even handle a criminal that had half a foot in the grave. We were supposed to bring him in alive, but because of me, Alice had to watch...as he killed the man she loves." Richard said as he hobbled away from Marc.

"You told me that you can't control certain things. This is one of them."

"When I went to the coroner's office and saw Phillip's burnt body lying there, I had to listen to what happened to him before he was killed. I had to step outside to recover. Marc… that piece of shit tortured him for over an hour and she couldn't do anything but watch. She couldn't get away, she couldn't fight, she couldn't call for help. I'm sorry. I have to go to work. We're getting the call log today which should help the case," Richard said as he packed his files, took his crutches and made his way out. Before leaving, Richard looked at Marc one last time.

"I love you more than you'll ever know," he said as he closed the door.

"I love you more than you'll ever know, too, you fool."

Marc walked to Alice's door and knocked.

"Are you okay? Do you need anything from me?" he asked, waiting for a reply.

She finally answered, "Come in."

Alice was sitting at a small desk working on Richard's computer surrounded by a bunch of paper on the floor.

"Sorry about the mess. Just take a seat anywhere," Alice said as she kept working.

Marc looked around and moved some papers off the bed and sat there, waiting for her to be done. Alice finally turned to face Marc. "I need a favor."

Marc was in shock, seeing Alice so calm. For a second, he worried that she was in denial again.

"It's funny how life is sometimes," she said as her thumb tapped her fingers in a rhythm. "I've been wondering why he isn't, on the wanted list. Why isn't he on the news? Why is it being kept a secret?"

"I did tell my boss that James was involved in the attack at the mayor's house, like you told me, but nothing happened. He said the police informed him not to publish any information about him," Marc stated.

"I checked the record and there was no contact between your boss and the police department."

"How do you know?"

"You and Richard were the first people that I talked to. I informed the chief after you told your boss," Alice answered.

That's when Marc noticed a picture of his boss next to him on the bed and picked it up.

"What is this?"

"If the police didn't tell your boss to stop the story, then who did?"

"Wait, do you think my boss is part of the cult?"

"I don't believe he has any relationship with them."

"Then, what are you seeing that I'm not?"

"Just a feeling."

"Please talk to me. I want to hear what you're thinking, what you're feeling. Someone in this house needs to talk."

"The night I killed Ethan, he had just jumped off a third-floor parking lot. That's not something a normal human can do."

"But didn't he get hurt from it? Richard told me that he was basically half dead."

"He was already hurt prior to the jump. How can a human go toe to toe against a Nova, get shot in the shoulder, jump off a third-floor parking lot and still give us a hard time?"

Marc started processing the information a bit. "But he's not a Nova."

"We all know the army experimented on the Novas when we took them in as refugees centuries ago."

"Every country did the same, except for Menea," Marc responded with a disturbed look.

"What if the army found a way to extract the Nova gene specific to strength?"

"But that's impossible."

"You know, for a journalist, you're quite the skeptic. All I'm asking is what if they found a way?"

"If they did, they would try to keep it a secret until they found a way to administer the gene without causing panic."

"Like keeping the police and the media quiet about it."

Marc looked shocked just thinking about the possibility. "Thinking that way is dangerous. You know they have killed for less. I can't help you get involved in this. I can't help you commit suicide."

"Sorry, it's my way of processing information. I need someone to bounce ideas off." Alice looked at the papers on the floor. "I do need help with something else though."

"As long as it has nothing to do with the army."

"Don't worry. Have you ever followed anyone before?"

"It's the nature of my job. Why do you ask?"

"I need you to follow someone for me."

Marc closed his eyes. "Who?" He couldn't say no to Alice after what she had gone through.

Alice pointed at a paper on the floor. "Him."

Marc picked up the paper. "Wait! Wait! This is a police officer."

"I know who he is already."

"You want me to tail an officer? Are you-" Marc stopped himself from finishing that sentence.

"Am I what? Crazy? No, on the contrary, I've never seen so clearly. Just because you can't see it, doesn't make me crazy."

"I didn't mean that. I'm sorry."

"Do I look so weak that you have to tiptoe around your words?"

"Of course not. I'm just worried about you."

"What I need right now is your help. Will you help me?"

Marc hesitated before answering and sighed. "What am I looking for?"

"See if there's anything suspicious about him."

"That's very vague. Is there something specific I'm looking for?"

"You're a journalist. I have a feeling you'll know."

A four-legged fluff ran in, leapt on the bed, and started rubbing her body on Alice's leg.

"I guess she missed you." Marc smiled.

Alice turned around and started typing.

Marc continued, "I was wondering when you'll be willing to see Myra, She's stopped by every day to check on you."

Alice sighed. "I'm sorry, but can I get some time to myself?"

"Oh, uhh, yeah, sorry, I'll leave."

"Can you also take her please?" Alice said looking at Nema.

"You know, she's been wanting to see you since you got here."

"Maybe in the future but not now, not yet."

Marc took the cat out with him.

As soon as Marc closed the door, Alice lifted up her laptop, revealing four files that had been hidden: Maxwell, Ethan, James, Myra. She touched Myra's file.

"I hope I'm wrong," Alice said as she continued to hear Nema meowing outside her door.

"I'm sorry, but I can't let go of this pain."

Chapter 23

James sat on his bed in his room at the Facility. He twisted the top of his necklace, releasing the smell of blood. He had just one regret about that night: that he couldn't hear them scream. But he did enjoy the look on Alice's face while begging him to stop. He looked at the vial.

"How do you like my hell, Alice? Soon you'll come to me to end it," he said to himself.

James heard the door open.

"What are you doing here? You're not supposed to be here this week," James asked Myra as she walked in.

Myra looked around. "Do you have anything to drink?"

"I have water."

Myra sighed. "Do you know why I'm here?"

James lay back on his pillow and closed his eyes. "Because I killed her husband. Didn't know you would care so much." He smiled.

Myra chuckled. "I came to say; 'great job.'"

James, taken aback by her words, opened his eyes and sat back up to look at her. "I didn't know you dabble in sarcasm."

"Because of you, Mother is moving again."

"What do you mean?"

"You revealed your identity. The police know who you are—but for some reason there's no wanted poster or report on the news about you. Why is that?"

"I knew she was powerful but never knew she was that influential. I guess she's really part of the military."

"Maybe."

"Why maybe?"

"Which country would you say is the most advanced?"

"Telsitius, obviously."

"Isn't it weird that a second-rate country like this created us?"

"You think Mother is a Teltius?"

Myra walks up to James and puts her hand on his shoulder. "Because of you, we will soon find out." She smiled.

"Since I was so helpful, I want something."

Myra smiled.

The following morning around five, Marc was in his car sipping his coffee in a thermo container. This was his third day following Jacob. Marc was a bit frustrated, because he couldn't see anything suspicious about him, but he wasn't about to stop. He needed to do this for Alice. He kept staring at his watch and waiting until finally he saw Jacob coming out of his house and getting into his car.

"All right, let's do this," he said to himself as he started his car. He knew that Jacob was heading to the precinct. Normally his biggest worry would be running into Richard, but today, Richard was at the doctor's getting his cast removed. He maintained his distance until he knew that Jacob had made it to the precinct.

Marc lingered outside the precinct waiting for anything suspicious until finally, Jacob came out of the precinct. He got in his car, and Marc followed. Jacob finally pulled in front of an old building in a shady neighborhood. He stayed in his car until someone came out of the building, and he went inside. Marc got out of his car and followed Jacob. He ran toward the closing door and pulled out a pen from his pocket and put it between the door to stop it from closing. He took a peek and saw Jacob going up the stairs. Marc opened the door and followed

Jacob up the stairs while trying to remain out of view. Jacob left the second floor and headed to the third. Marc started going up the stairs while trying to make as little sound as possible. Jacob stopped on the third floor and looked down. He shrugged and stepped into the third floor hallway.

Marc was hiding right below Jacob, flat against the wall. When he was sure that Jacob was in the hallway, he started moving again. On the third floor, Marc heard a loud sound from the hallway and took a peek to see an open door. Some residents came out to check what was going on. Marc quickly pulled out his phone to take advantage of the situation. Since people were out, he could easily look like he lived in the building and just wanted to check what was going on. As Marc walked past the open door, Jacob came out with a cuffed man and their eyes met for the first time. Marc didn't stop and kept walking while holding his phone upside-down to film the inside.

"Stop!" Jacob yelled at Marc.

Crap, crap, crap, does he know? Mark thought to himself as he turned around to face Jacob.

"Is there a problem, Officer?"

"Yeah, those shoes are way too nice. Where did you get them?" Jacob laughed.

"Oh, they were actually a gift, so I don't know. Sorry."

"That's too bad. Do you know what shoes these are?" Jacob asked the cuffed man.

"They're one of Roloro's limited editions," The man answered.

"You see, that's why you always ask a counterfeit expert. Well enjoy the rest of your day. There will be some officers arriving soon so don't mind the noise," Jacob said to Marc as he walked away with the arrested man.

Marc kept walking until he got to the other side of the hallway where he wasn't visible and leaned on the wall. He touched his chest, trying to calm his heart. After a couple minutes passed, he was quickly back on Jacob's tail and followed him back to the precinct. Marc parked far away and waited for Jacob's next move.

An hour had passed. Marc was tired, and he had nothing on Jacob. He wanted to help Alice, but he was starting to wonder if this was just crazy. He took a sip of coffee and heard a knock. It was Jacob, tapping the car window with his gun. Marc dropped his coffee on the car floor and lowered the car window slowly. Jacob leaned in, close to his face.

"Hello fancy shoes—or do you prefer Marc?"

"I think you have the wrong person," Marc responded in fear.

"You think so? Maybe you're right. Why don't I go to Richard and ask him why his boyfriend has been following me?"

"Wait!"

"That's what I thought. Now unlock the back. I always wanted a chauffeur." He smiled as he got in the back of the car and kept his gun pointed at Marc.

"What are you going to do to me?"

"Don't worry, I'm just going to take you for a ride. Start driving." Marc turned the car on and started driving.

"When did you find out about me?" Marc asked.

"We always knew about you."

"We?"

"Our bosses are well informed," Jacob stated.

"Don't you mean your gods?"

"Doesn't Richard know not to share case information?"

"So, it is a cult. You must be smart enough to know that you're being used."

"I'm being used every day when I go to work, and the same applies to you. You get used for money. We all set our price in life and the price I set was more than money."

"Even at the cost of innocent people."

"Innocent people die every day. Our military kills people that they deem traitors to this country. Why is it that they're allowed to kill people by just branding them as traitors?"

"That doesn't justify it."

"The truth is, I don't care anymore. I lost the people that matter most to me so I could give you a bunch of reasons why it's our right to kill anyone we want, but the reality is when you're in that dark hole all by yourself, your basic instinct is to ask why you. You start looking for reason, but there's no reason. There's no higher power keeping you safe, and if there's no higher power up there, then I might as well take the hand of the devil that I know is there in my darkest moment."

Marc looked in his rearview mirror to see a sad look on Jacob's face. "I'm sorry you feel that no one was there when you needed them. But that's still no reason."

"How's Alice doing by the way?"

"Better than you, because she got her friends there for her."

"You think so? I bet you she's not. It is easy to fool people with a smile in times of distress, because the same people that are trying to help you are the ones looking for a smile to make them feel like they are achieving something. When you lose the people that you love, it changes you."

"She's going through this because of you." Said Marc.

"She's going through this because she wasn't strong enough to protect the people that she loved, but soon that weakness will be taken away."

"Are you fucking serious?" Marc stepped on the brakes and turned around to face Jacob "Don't you even dare! You did the same thing that was done to you. You're nothing more than a hypocrite!"

"Enough! You're blocking the street and making a scene. If you don't start driving, then Richard might have an accident. So, take the next left," Jacob said sternly.

"No," he replied with a shaken voice.

"Now, take the left like I asked."

Marc complied with his demands. He was driving through the factory district when Jacob asked him to turn into an abandoned factory lot and park the car.

"So, this is where you all have been hiding?" Marc asked.

Marc pulled out a small tube out of his pocket.

"Put it on," Jacob said while he pointed his gun at Marc's temple.

He complied with Jacob's demand and put the cream on. "Is this a skincare cult or a murder cult?"

Jacob smiled and got closer to Marc. "Let me guess: a guy with a gun is just looking to feel big, and the only way he can feel big is by seeing the fear in your eyes, so always add some humor when you can to remind him of how insignificant he is. Is that what Richard taught you?"

"I don't know what you're talking about."

"I guess not, because you're funnier than your boyfriend," Jacob said as he started laughing loudly and got out of the car.

Marc still had a gun pointed at him as he got out of the car and stared at the abandoned factory.

"Come on. Let's go," Jacob said as he pointed away from the abandoned factory.

They walked for a couple of minutes before reaching another abandoned factory. Marc looked behind him and could see the other abandoned building that he had parked the car at.

"Why didn't we park here?"

"We have a big meeting today with our gods. We leave this area empty for them."

Marc saw a homeless person laying on the floor in front of the factory and their eyes met. Marc started sending him signals with his eyes. The homeless man got up and started walking their way.

"Are you okay?" the man asked as he got closer to them.

"Yes, we are fine," Jacob quickly answered.

Marc kept trying to send the homeless man signals without letting Jacob notice, when he heard Jacob laughing from behind.

"Sorry, I can't believe you fell for it," Jacob said while laughing.

"What's going on?" Marc yelled.

When the door to the factory opened, he saw James walk out. "Welcome to our workshop," James said with his arms open as he came down the small steps.

Both Jacob and the homeless man bowed down before James. This was Marc's chance to try to run away. He was waiting for this moment. He put one foot in front of the other and with all his strength swung his fists at James and kept swinging. His rage overtook him, making it impossible for him to run away.

"It's your fault!" Marc yelled while rushing at James.

Jacob and the homeless man quickly got up to stop Marc, but James had already grabbed Marc by the neck and brought him to his knees.

"Do you know I strangled her with the same hand that's strangling you right now right before making her watched?" James said as he felt Marc's pulse through his neck. With every squeeze he felt Marc's heart beating faster until finally releasing him. James watched as he rolled on the floor gasping for air. Marc could feel his heart beating out of his chest. Trying to breathe with all his might, he took a glance at James and could tell that all his hits hadn't left a scratch. Marc could see the entrance to the factory open wide in front of him. He knew that if he didn't escape, he would die today, and he would never see Richard again. He had to try. Marc summoned the strength to get up and turned to face James.

"That's all you got? Strength and nothing else? A lot of good that did Ethan." He lifted his fist. *How can I ever look at Alice in the eyes if I run away now?*

James got face to face with Marc. "If you're trying to force me to kill you out of rage then you're sorely mistaken because I plan to enjoy every second of this," James said as he headbutted Marc to the ground and knocked him out. James lifted him up and sniffed the blood gushing out of Marc's head.

"Oh no, we can't have this going to waste now," James said as he called the homeless man over. "Stop the bleeding and take him to my room."

James headed back inside while the homeless man carried Marc, leaving Jacob outside by himself. "I'm sorry," he said to the ground where Marc had been. He headed back to Marc's car, all the while thinking about what he had done, everything he had sacrificed so he would never have to feel that pain again. When he got to the car, he paused before opening the door. Then everything went dark.

Chapter 24

Earlier, Richard was at the doctor's office to remove the nano cast.

"All right, let's get this off so you can be on your way," the doctor said to Richard.

"If I didn't know better, I would say you're trying to get rid of me."

"Of course not. I just have a lot of patients to take care of." The doctor put on a black glove with blue light on the back. As he passed his hand over the cast, a black smoke came out of the cast and went directly in the glove. The doctor took the glove off and put it in a secure container.

"It always blows my mind when I see their technology," Richard said as he wiggled his foot.

"This is nothing. The Teltius have the technology to cure your broken leg in a day."

"Why don't they share that with us?"

The doctor flicks Richards' leg. "Do you know why I'm in a hurry?"

"To help other patients, like you said."

"Yes, to make up for the soldiers that we sacrificed for this technology. If I can save more lives than the amount being lost in this war, then maybe it would be worth it. So, I always have to be in a hurry, because that number is always increasing," the doctor answered.

"Sorry, I've been stressed a lot lately, so I ramble sometimes without thinking."

"Well now you can go ramble to someone else because you're good to go, and please let me not see you for a long time." The doctor smiled as he left the room.

Would it have made a difference if my leg was healed in one day? Richard questioned himself as he left the doctor's office and headed to the precinct.

As soon as Richard got to the precinct, he was called to the chief's office.

"I see you're back on your feet," the chief said to him as he walked in.

"I am. And ready to jump back in the field."

"That's good to hear. How is she doing?" the chief asked.

"I honestly don't know. She's been stuck in her room the entire time."

"You need to push your way in. The worst thing right now is to leave her alone with her thoughts."

"I know. But I also don't want to push her too hard if she's not ready."

The chief rubbed his eyes as he sighed. "I spoke to the coroner. He said he should be able to release the body by next week."

"Thank you. She needs this."

"You need to remind her that we are here for her. We will take care of everything for her. She doesn't need to worry about the cost."

Richard smiled. "Thank you."

"If you really want to thank me, get that son of a bitch," the chief said with a stern look.

"If I'm going to capture James, I want to know: why we are keeping his information low profile?"

The chief looked around before answering. "I'm not supposed to say this, but the military reached out to me a couple of days ago."

"Let me guess, they want to keep James out of the public sight."

The chief raised his eyebrow. "That is correct. How did you know?"

"It was just a guess. After what happened to Alice, there's no way you would do everything in your power to catch him. There's only one reason you wouldn't put his face out there in the public… the military."

"Then, why ask?"

"It was just a passing thought. I didn't have anyone to bounce it off, so I wasn't 100% sure."

"Are you going to be able to do this without her?"

"I will do this because of her."

"There's another reason I called you in."

"What is it?" Richard asked.

"I got the call log from our three suspects, and Jacob's number wasn't on it."

"Are you sure!?"

"All three of them received a call before you got there, and it was from an unregistered number."

"So, it could have still been Jacob," Richard said as he clenched his fist.

"But if you don't have any proof, we can't do anything to him."

"I've always been able to catch my suspects. This time won't be no different."

"That's what I want to hear. Do you have a plan?"

"Kind of."

"What is it?"

"Sending someone I don't want to. To tail him."

"He'll know that someone is tailing him. He's one of our best officers."

"That's the plan. So far, we assume it's a big group, but weirdly enough the only ones doing the killing have been their leaders."

"You want to use someone as bait."

"If he finds someone is tailing him, he would most likely take that person back to their base."

"That's a lot of guessing. Why would he take that chance?"

"He won't have a choice. If we use the right bait."

"I take it you know what bait to use?"

"Sadly, yes."

The chief took a look out of his office and turned to face Richard. "Since he's not here right now, start setting everything up and tell me if you need anything."

"Will do," Richard said as he got up and left the chief's office.

Richard went directly to the restroom where he splashed water on his face. He looked at himself in the mirror. *So, this is how I look right now.*

He knew that this was his lowest moment, somewhere he had never been in. Richard pulled out his phone and looked at Marc's number. *Am I really going to do this?*

He called Marc and waited for him to answer. *What am I going to say?*

"Hi, you've reached Ma-" Richard hung up and dialed Marc's number again. Again, it went straight to his voicemail.

Richard put his phone back in his pocket and turned the water on again to splash his face. *Why is this so hard?* Richard took his phone out again and called Alice. The phone rang for a couple of seconds before Alice picked up.

"How are you doing?" Richard asked.

"I… don't know?"

"I'm here for you to listen and help you when you're sad, when you're angry. You know that, right?"

"How's the case going?" Alice asked, switching the conversation.

"You know I can't tell you that."

"So, I take it that Jacob's number didn't pop up in the suspect's call log?"

"What makes you say that?"

"I've worked with you long enough to know that if his number had popped up, you would have either been suspended or put him in jail."

"How do you know I didn't put him in jail?"

"Because the only reason you wouldn't attack him is because you would want me to look him in his eyes and see if I can break him for information. Create a connection between him and I about how we both lost people that we love."

"On the plus side, I have a backup plan."

"I bet you do," Alice responded with a gentle voice, giving Richard hope that she was doing better.

"Have you seen Marc? I can't reach him."

"I haven't seen him since this morning. He said he had a job to do and left."

"It's fine. I'll talk to him when I get home."

"Sorry, Richard, but I have to go. I think Myra's at the door."

"Oh, before you go."

Before Richard could finish his sentence, Alice had already hung up on him.

"The chief got his body released early so we will need to make preparations," Richard continued as he looked at his phone looking defeated.

Alice put her phone back in her pocket while staring at the other abandoned factory that Marc was taken to before turning around.

"Sorry about that," Alice said as she got close to a tied-up Jacob and removed his gag.

"What's going on?" Jacob yelled before being punched by Alice.

"No 'Hi, Alice' or 'How are you doing, Alice'?" Alice smiled as she punched him for the second time.

"Have you lost your damn mind?" Jacob asked with a bloody mouth.

"Not really. I wasn't planning on hitting you but seeing your face just brings up this burning rage inside me!" Alice said with a vivid smile while gripping at Jacob's face, her nails digging through his skin.

"Wait, Alice, we work together-" Alice landed another punch on Jacob's jaw.

"Richard had a theory that when you saw me, you would be overwhelmed with guilt for helping James do exactly what happened to you, so you would confess, but I know now that will never happen because now that I'm in your shoes, nothing will deter me from my goal."

Jacob looked at Alice and all he could see was her rage. "You look like my reflection from back then."

"Why?"

"Does it matter?"

"No, it doesn't," Alice answered as she undid her fist.

"How did you find me?"

"I set a tracker on his car, waiting for you to act."

"How did you know I was going to kidnap Marc?"

"James told me, 'Welcome to my hell'. I took a guess that he would want me to keep suffering by killing those close to me."

Jacob laughed. "I can't believe I didn't see that coming."

Alice gripped his face with all her strength and got close enough that he could feel her breath. "You couldn't see it, because you lost this rage!" she growled as she smashed Jacob to the floor, breaking the chair that he was tied to.

His head was ringing and still had the rope around him, which he quickly tried to get out of.

"Take your time. I'm not going anywhere." Alice walked around him and set herself up at the exit.

"You are no different from me. Didn't you send Marc to his death?" Jacob said as he got himself out of the rope and got up.

"I'll save him."

Jacob wiped the blood off his face. He stood in front of Alice. If he could bring her to James, surely, they would reward him. At the same time, he knew that Alice was the person who was able to go toe to toe with Ethan. He had to take the risk and throw her off balance somehow. And it hit him.

"Since you came by yourself, I guess it never occurred to you that you will just end up seeing someone you care about get killed. Poor Marc." Jacob smiled showing his bloody teeth.

"Who was it that died first? Your daughter or your wife?"

"Shut up!"

"Did she cry, 'Daddy help-'"

"I said shut up." Jacob yelled as he rushed at Alice.

In that split second, one thought came to her mind. *You should use your environment as a weapon.* She stepped on a metal pipe laying on the floor by her feet, sending it in the air above her. Using all her strength, she grabbed it in midair and slammed it down on Jacob's shoulder. She could hear the sound of his bone breaking as he fell to his knees, screaming in pain. The blow leaving an indentation of the pipe on his shoulder.

"You know, the other people in your cult I can understand, but you? You went after one of your own! We were your other family! And you think you can throw me off my game by mentioning my dead husband," Alice said as she walked past him and to the windows where she could see the factory where she could end everything.

Jacob was in an incredible amount of pain. Any movement sent pain throughout his whole body.

"What do you want with me?" he asked.

"Honestly? I really want to kill you right now, but I think letting you live in your own hell is more appropriate."

"Are you going to call for backup and tell them what I've done?"

"Even now you're so self-centered. Well, who I'm I to talk right this moment? I'm debating whether to call for backup or just wait for him to come out and have him all to myself."

"If you call for backup, you won't be able to torture him, you mean." Jacob sat against the wall facing her, already knowing he was defeated.

"Don't worry. I'll be giving up the badge. People like you and me with so much rage in us should never hold the badge."

"Too bad I couldn't see it that way."

"Have you ever heard of a person named Myra?"

Jacob took a second before he answered. "No. Why?"

Alice ground her teeth out of rage. She threw the pipe with all her strength at the wall. The pipe made a loud sound on impact and rolled between the two of them. Alice turned toward Jacob, breathing heavily. "Why are you lying?"

"I'm not lying!"

Alice took a couple of breaths. "I know you've been gathering information on Richard and me. You definitely know who she is. So why lie about it? Because she's your fourth leader. Isn't she?"

"You'll have to go to find out."

Alice turned back to look at the factory and touched her neck lightly. "I don't need to. I already know."

"Too much drama." An unknown voice came from behind Jacob. Alice turned around to see a man snapping Jacob's neck and watched him fall to the floor.

Chapter 25

Alice rushed toward the man, kicking the metal pipe on the floor toward his head. Without faltering, he caught the pipe in mid-air. Alice followed with her fist heading straight for the man's head. Right when she was about to land her blow, she was stopped.

"Why is Mother interested in a Lesser like you?" a woman said as she gripped Alice's wrist.

She was so focused on the man that had killed Jacob, that she hadn't seen the woman that stood near him. Alice couldn't move her hand but didn't let that stop her and quickly attacked the back of the woman's knee with her leg, causing the unknown woman to buckle and release her grip on Alice. Who quickly threw a punch, trying to knock her off balance. The woman used her other hand to grab Alice's fist.

"Sneaky," the woman said. She started crushing Alice's fist with her hand, bringing Alice to her knees.

"Mother said not to hurt her," the man said, and the woman released Alice. She pulled out a cigarette and lit it up, visibly annoyed. "Who are you? Do you work for Myra and Maxwell? Is Myra Mother? Is that what you call her?" Alice opened and closed her fist, trying to regain feeling in her hand.

The woman started laughing and the man smirked. "You shouldn't ask so many questions."

"I should at least know who I'm talking to."

"You're talking to your superiors," the woman answered.

"I didn't realize that my superiors needed to team up against a lowly 'Lesser' like me."

The man's expression wrenched with anger. The woman exhaled the smoke in his face and turned to Alice.

"Forgive my brother. He's not used to talking to a Lesser that's so disrespectful. You'd be surprised how often people beg for us to spare them but not you. I like that!"

Alice was at a loss. She had thought the man was the calm one and the woman was the crazy one.

"I take it James called you a Lesser when he was killing your husband," the man said as he regained his composure.

"He didn't just kill my husband, he-"

"Don't care. You're starting to bore me with this conversation. I have one question for you. What do you intend to do to James?" the woman asked.

Alice hesitated and answered. "Kill him."

"I doubt you can," the man said.

The woman offered a hand to Alice and helped her up her feet. "I would love for you to kill him," she said to Alice.

"I thought you worked together." Alice said.

"We used to be a family. If you can call it that," he answered.

"What if I told you that we'll help you get your revenge?" the woman said as she took a puff.

"Why would you help me kill your own family member?"

"If you can kill him, then he never deserved to be part of our family."

"You're using me to test your little project. I take it that the one you call Mother is in charge."

"She's smarter than I thought," the man said, looking at his partner.

"What little project do you think we are using you for?"

"It's not that hard to guess that the army has been experimenting on Novas all over again and they finally succeeded-"

"Why the hell are we just letting her talk?!" The man yelled.

The woman exhaled a puff of smoke in the man's face for the second time and handed him her cigarette pack. "Take one and take a break." She said with a smile.

"I'm fine."

The woman wiped the smile off her face. "I said take one and take a break," the woman said in a stern voice.

The man took a cigarette and walked to the window.

"Sorry about that. Go on," she said with the eerie smile back on her face.

Alice tried to take a step back before the woman grabbed her by the shoulder.

"Go on."

"You're experimenting with Nova genes."

"Hmmm, I need to ask Mother if that is the case. You know, she never actually told us."

"And you never told me your names."

"Oh my God!" The woman tapped her own forehead, as she released Alice's shoulder. "How could I be so rude? Sorry about that. We've never talked so much to a Lesser before. No social skills whatsoever." The woman laughed. "I'm Michelle and the grump over there is Luther."

"And what's with the smoking in his face?" Alice asked.

"How do I say this without being rude… Oh!" she said as she slammed her fist in her palm. "The smell of cigarettes overpowers your stench."

Alice sniffed herself.

"I mean I could rip you open to get rid of the smell, but Mother would not be happy."

"So Mother is the one I have to thank for James."

"Actually, that would be Myra. She set everything up and chose you and Richard as her target."

"But why us?"

"Attention," Luther said while smoking.

"Attention! All this shit for attention?"

"The need to be validated pushes people to the extreme."

"Of course, you would know." Luther smirked at Michelle, who then picked up the metal pipe on the floor and threw it at his face. Luther dodged the pipe and let it penetrate the wall by his head.

"Don't you know it's rude to interrupt?" Michelle smirked at Luther, who pulled out the metal pipe from the wall and looked at it. "I'll hold on to this for now since my face seems to have a target painted on it."

Michelle turned to Alice. "Here's the deal. You kill James and you get to live… maybe. Or, hear me out on this one! I just kill you here and now."

As Alice was about to answer, Michelle stopped her by putting her finger in front of Alice's mouth and took her last puff before throwing her cigarette on the floor and exhaling.

"Sorry I like to enjoy the last one."

Luther started laughing out loud. Alice moved Michelle's hands away from her face. "I'm going to do more than kill James. I'm going to kill them all and leave Myra for last."

"Well said! I mean, I would much rather gut you and Myra together, but hey, what can you do?"

Luther put his cigarette out and walked back to them.

"So, how much backup do you have on your side?" Alice asked.

"Backup? We are the backup. What? You want us to bring more people to steal our fun? No, thank you."

"Okay, so what's the plan?"

"Oh, simple. We walk in and start killing."

"Are you crazy? We don't know how many people are inside, and I'm not going to kill anyone but those three."

"Wait! You thought we were going to share the kill?" Michelle started laughing. "Talk about selfishness. We'll take care of everything. You just worry about James."

"I have a friend inside, and I want to save him."

Luther exhaled. "Seriously?"

"Sorry, we aren't in the life saving business. Well, maybe we are, since we just saved your life by not killing you. You should be more thankful to us."

"I need to save him." Alice pushed back.

"I guess if he doesn't attack us, we won't have to kill him. Oh, my God. This must be how it feels to be good." Michelle eerily smiled. "Iiiii doonnn't liiiike itttt."

"Don't worry. You won't be saving anyone. I'll do it myself."

"Are you ready for the reunion?" Luther said, looking at Michelle who cracked her neck.

"What are we waiting for? Let's go."

"Are we really just going to walk in the front door?" Alice asked.

"I guess she didn't notice," Michelle said as she walked to the window.

"Well, that's to be expected. Detective, didn't you notice anything on your drive here?"

"Like what?"

"That there hasn't been one single car that drove by since you got here."

"Did you guys block the streets?"

"Too obvious... we just had our people change the navigation system for every car. That way, the GPS is always avoiding this area," Luther replied.

"Okay, so, what does that have to do with us going through the front door?"

"What's the point of sneaking around if they know we are coming?" Michelle replied while staring through the window.

"Wait! They know we are coming."

"Maxwell arrived before we set this up, so he might not have noticed," Luther answered.

"But Myra just arrived. There's no way she wouldn't. Well, then again, she does know how to disappoint, wouldn't you say?" Michelle said while twisting her neck back to look at Myra, who had just arrived at the facility.

"The only thing I'm interested in is killing them."

"So scary! I hope she doesn't try to kill us." Michelle giggled at Luther, who took off his tie and blazer and threw, both on the ground. He rolled his shirt sleeves up.

"Now, that's better. Going to need to move freely." He rested the metal pipe on his shoulder.

Alice looked at Jacob's dead body on the floor before following behind them.

The trio stood in front of the facility, the two of them in the front and Alice following. The second the homeless man caught a glimpse of them, he started walking toward them with an empty bowl, begging for money. When he got close to Michelle, he pulled out a knife from his bowl. Michelle easily grabbed his knife wielding hand, broke it and forced the man to stab his own face.

"Oops, I didn't catch that." Michelle smiled as she grabbed the dead man by his neck and tossed him to Luther, who kicked the body towards the door and broke it open.

"Now that's how we do our entrance." Luther smiled.

Chapter 26

Prior to the assault on the facility, Maxwell was reading in his room when Elaine came in. "Sorry I'm late. I wanted to make sure no one was following me."

Maxwell closed the book, pulled Elaine into his arms, and kissed her. "You never need to explain anything to me."

"I'm just telling you about my day," Elaine responded while giggling.

"We aren't normal, are we?"

"What part? The killer couple or the cult following?"

"Hey! The cult brought me to you," Maxwell said with a smile.

Elaine laid her head on his chest. "It's the other way around, it brought me to you."

"You truly are the most amazing woman on this planet. When I'm with you, the world is no longer gray—and I don't need to paint it red to bring it to life anymore."

"How can I not love you when you look at me with those eyes? You might have been a weapon, but now you're my husband and I'll make sure to tell Mother that when I see her."

Maxwell started laughing at Elaine. "Sorry about that. I just pictured you talking to Mother."

"Are you making fun of me?"

"I guess I can never stop being bad." Maxwell smiled. As he was about to kiss her, he smelled blood coming from the hallway.

Maxwell opened the door and saw James walking by with blood on his knuckles.

"What's going on?" Maxwell asked.

"I got us a fun toy for tonight's meeting."

"What did you do?"

"Nothing. A bird just came in flying through our window. I had to take care of it."

"James, who's this bird?" Maxwell asked sternly.

"Look who thinks he's in charge," James said as he poked Maxwell, leaving a small blood stain on his shirt. "Oops."

Maxwell moved his brother's finger away. "All three of us are in charge. I just want to make sure you're not doing anything crazy."

"All three of us? It didn't take that long for you to change the verbiage. It used to be four of us. At least Myra knows how to fake it."

"James... I don't know how to handle our brother's loss. We were never taught how to. You know I loved him."

"Really? I wonder if you would react the same way if your wife died."

Maxwell slammed James to the wall. "Don't you even dare!" Maxwell's voice thundered in the hallway. Elaine rushed out to try to calm him down.

James smiled at Maxwell. "Where has that side of you been?" he said as he pushed Maxwell's hands off him.

"It's not what you think," Maxwell said, trying to justify himself.

"That you value a Lesser over your own brother. Of course not, anyway I need to go back to my room." James took a couple of steps before turning back to face Maxwell and Elaine. "By the way, my dear sister-in-law, you would do well to put your cream on before our sister gets here," he said as he left them.

Maxwell turned to Elaine.

"I'm so sorry! I didn't mean to not put it on." Elaine pleaded.

Maxwell slid his hand into hers and guided her back to his room. "You have nothing to apologize for. I should have reminded you. I guess I don't notice anymore," Maxwell said as he put on a sad smile.

Elaine's warm hand touched his cheeks, trying to comfort him. "Why that face?" she asked.

"Do you even see me as your husband?"

"From the day I said I do. I know that sometimes I make it hard to see that when we are in the facility, but you, more than anyone else, should know that I need to keep up appearances." She smiled.

"Why do you make me act like a fool?"

"Does that mean I turned a god into a fool?"

"Court jester, at your service," Maxwell bowed.

"We still need to work on your humor." Elaine laughed.

"I'm working on it. Hey, do you know why seven doesn't like nine?

"No, can you tell me?"

"Apparently, because seven hate nine," Maxwell said with anticipation.

"Oh, honey, it's seven ate nine." She wrapped her arms around his neck and smiled. "You don't get why it's funny do you?"

"Not really, but I heard it's a good beginner's joke."

"You mean it's a good dad joke," she whispered under her breath.

"I'm sorry," he whispered.

"Why don't you help me put on the cream?" she changed the subject.

"Sure."

James paused inside his room, thinking about his interaction with Maxwell. Then he walked to his private fitness room where Marc was passed out on the floor. He stooped down to Marc's level.

"How to wake you up? I guess I could use water. Or, I could just do this," James said as he broke one of Marc's fingers. Marc screamed in pain. "Well, hello there." James smiled.

Marc looked around him, holding his hand to his chest. "Where am I?!"

James spun around. "You're in my private room."

"The police know where I am. Let me go now and you won't get hurt."

James slammed Marc's head to the floor, reopening his head wound. "What difference does it make whether they know where we are? To be frank with you, I hope they do know!"

Marc could barely make out what James was saying. "What are you going to do to me?" he mumbled.

"You know how you need to tenderize the meat before you cook it to make sure that it is nice and juicy?"

"So, you're going to torture me? How original," Marc said, before being punched in the face.

"You know, it's hard for me not to kill you. With every punch I need to make sure I'm controlling my strength; otherwise, I might kill you too early. So, if you wouldn't mind not being an ass, that would be great."

"Sorry, I can't seem to control my mouth when I'm in front of a baby that constantly cries about his dead brother," Marc said as he got up to face James.

"A baby. Let's see if we can change that." James punched Marc and sent him crashing into the floor. That's when Marc realized that he hadn't been lying about holding back. It took all of Marc's willpower to not pass out. He thought about Richard and how he wished he could see him again when he felt James's grip around his wrist.

"I believe you need this hand to write. Since this is your last day as a journalist, you won't have to worry about the loss," James said, as he released his full force and easily crushed every bone in Marc's right hand. Some bone stuck out of his skin. The pain was unbearable. Marc let out a blistering scream, grinding his teeth, spit flying out of his mouth. He clawed at the floor and tried to distance himself from the pain by thinking of Richard, but it was too much.

James took a knee. "Damn, you're really trying to keep it in. Good thing your backup is coming, so you'll be fine once they take you to the hospital." James got closer to him. "Marc, are you listening? Maarrrccc, earth to Marc."

Marc was in so much pain he couldn't hear him. James held down Marc's broken hand and stared at the small piece of bone sticking out.

"Marc, don't you know it's rude to ignore someone when they're talking to you." James said as he grabbed the piece of bone sticking out between Marc's two fingers and pulled it out, making Marc scream even louder in pain with all his might.

What is this hell? Marc thought as he held his broken hand in agony.

James picked at his ear. "Can you not yell that loud? I have neighbors." James smirked.   He could tell that Marc was in the process of passing out, so he slapped him in the face.   "Hey! Come on. We're just starting. You can't be passing out on me for a second time. Phillip

313

lasted a bit longer than that. I wonder if it was because the person he loved was in front of him." James thought about it for a second. "I wonder if you'll last longer if I bring Richard in to watch the fun."

James started laughing before Marc slowly moved his trembling hand, mustering up all his strength to grab James by the collar. "Don't.. you… dare."

James brushed off his hand and grabbed him by the shoulder. "I guess we have more in common than I thought. I never thought that a Lesser could care the way we do, you know." James leaned Marc against the wall.

"Does that mean you're going to let me live?"

Without smiling or batting an eyelash, he stared straight at Marc without saying a word before stepping away.

Marc almost wished that James had said something instead of giving him that look. James came back with a small box and sat in front of Marc. He opened the box, revealing three vials. He pulled out one of the vials and looked at it.

"I've killed a lot of people in my life, but she was special. Do you know that as my brother and I were about to kill her, she smiled at us? There was no fear in her eyes."

Marc ground his teeth. "You won't find any fear in mine."

"When we asked her why she was smiling, she said, death is inevitable—so why should she fear it? And that the truly sad thing is that we were keeping our looks away from the world."

"So, you remember her because she commented on your looks?" Marc said, sweating profusely.

"We remember her because she reminded us of Mother, both focused on their jobs to the point of death, and we think that is beautiful."

"Who's Mother?"

"We found out that the woman worked for a modeling agency and that is when our career started," James kept talking, ignoring Marc's questions.

James pulled out the second vial. "This is Ethan. We have each other's blood, so that we would never be without each other again."

"Why are you telling me this?"

James kept staring at Ethan's blood vial. "You would do anything for those you care about. I never understood that feeling. I guess it's because I never thought anything could ever happen to us—but now, I realize I had those feelings for as long as I remember. I can remember when I first opened my eyes. He was in the opposite pod from mine. We opened our eyes at the same time and saw each other. The first time we moved our body in the cold water was to reach out to each other. For a while, we thought we were the only two people in this world. I don't know if we are truly brothers, but I know that we were always there for each other, until now." James paused for a second as he looked at the vial.

"You know, you're doing the same thing that happened to you."

"That is the inner turmoil I'm dealing with. I was taught that it's my right to kill any lesser that I please, because they are the past, because they are weak." James remembered Alice's words for a second before continuing "But now... what does it make him?"

"A human that breathes, that has memories, people he cares about but also people who care for him when he's gone, like everyone that you've killed," Marc mumbled.

James put the vial of blood back in the box and picked up the last one.

"When I tortured Phillip in front of Alice, it was like looking in a mirror. For a second the rage stopped, and that's when I realized I couldn't kill her."

Marc realized what was in the vial that he was looking at. "You bastard." He spat in James's face, and James easily dodged it.

"And here I thought we were connecting. But what you're feeling right now is nothing compared to my burning hatred!" James said, with rage in his eyes. "I will keep killing everyone that Alice loves, until the day she comes to me and begs me to kill her, and I will say no, because every second of misery she feels is a second of relief for me."

Marc started laughing at James.

"Good to know that you still have the energy to laugh."

"Sorry. It's just that she will kill you, because you aren't as special as you think you are. So be scared, because every second you're alive is a second that she will be coming after you. For the rest of your life, you will be running away from her, because you are a coward who can only get his goons to do his dirty work and attack from behind just like a filthy rat! You can kill me today, but she will kill you sooner or later."

James put the vials back in the box and closed it, staring at Marc with a smile.

"This is why I like you; you don't break easily. But the more you struggle, the more I look forward to breaking you." James grabbed Marc's left hand. "You know, I've always been curious to see if I could crush someone's bone in my hand Let's give it a try."

Marc breathed heavily and closed his eyes. James had destroyed his right hand and was about to do the same to his left hand. He could hear his bones cracking under

James' pressure. Marc started sweating, his heart beating harder. A second felt like an eternity for him as he felt James's squeeze getting stronger. He could tell his bone was about to be permanently broken when James heard a knock on his door and released his grip.

"Sorry, I need to see who's interrupting me," James said as he stood up and turned, which left Marc with a sense of relief, but then James turned to face Marc again.

"I can't believe I almost forgot," James said. He stomped on Marc's leg, breaking it.

Marc screamed trying to hold his leg but unable to. All he could do to fight the pain was bang his head repeatedly on the wall behind him.

James opened the door to see Myra. "Hey, sis."

"Seems I'm interrupting," Myra said as she made her way in.

"What do you want?"

"I came to tell you we need to prepare ourselves. Mother's coming."

"How do you know?"

"Help me!! Please help me!!" Marc pleaded.

Myra turned and went through James's fitness room and saw Marc crying in pain.

"Myra! What are you doing here?"

"Hi, Marc. How have you been?"

"Help me!" Marc begged, as he heard James laughing in the corner.

"Sis, aren't you going to help him?" James kept laughing as he saw the look on Marc change from hope to despair.

"What happened to the cheery Marc that I know and love?" Myra said with a curious face.

"We trusted you!"

"I would hope so. I put a lot of effort into making you guys trust me."

It was the first time that Marc stopped shaking from the pain. Instead, it was fear that had taken over. Tears running down his face, he stared at Myra and begged her.

"Please! Don't ever let Alice find out."

"Find out what, I wonder?" Myra said looking at James.

"I'm getting good at this emotional thing. I would guess how amazing we are." James smiled.

"Please don't let her find out that you lied to her." Marc begged.

"Oh. You mean don't let her know that the culprit she was looking for was right next to her the whole time?"

"Please don't."

"Damn it! I guess I got it wrong," James said to himself as he snapped his finger.

"Marc, you and Alice are some of my favorite Lessers, but I couldn't care less about either of you."

"He's forcing you to say that to break me. It'll be fine .We'll make it out of here." Marc said to Myra with tears running down his face.

Myra faced his brother. "And that's how you break someone."

"You're ruining my fun."

"Your fun can wait. We need to get ready for Mother," Myra said.

"Do you have a plan?" James asked as he followed her down the hallway.

"I figure she will send Luther and Michelle. We'll direct everyone in the facility to the entrance as a welcome party for our lovely brother and sister "

"Do you think they're working for her?"

"Without a doubt. Her perfect creations."

"Those two are monsters, the best of us."

"We've grown. We are not the same kids we used to be."

"So have they," James said.

"Good thing we've been preparing for this," she said, as she knocked on Maxwell's door.

"Can we do this?"

"We're about to find out."

Elaine opened the door.

"Uhh, I can't help but recall saying everyone is supposed to go upstairs. That includes you too." Myra looked at Elaine.

"I told her to stay by my side," Maxwell answered.

"What is wrong with you?" James asked him.

"Now, now, our brother and sister are on their way here. We can't be arguing with each other right now." Myra intervened.

"Will you even be able to fight if she's by your side?" James asked.

"When the time comes, she will be staying here where it's safe."

"While we put our lives at risk." James stated as he saw a man running toward them.

"Three people just smashed through the entrance upstairs. We need your help my gods!" the man said, panting.

James without missing a beat, grabbed the man by his neck and snapped it.

"What did you do!?" Elaine yelled.

"I snapped his neck."

"But he's one of us."

"He's one of you!" James snarled.

"Watch your tone!" Maxwell barked at James.

Myra got between both of them. "Enough! I am not Mother. I will not be handling children, so get over your shit right this second, and let's go deal with our siblings upstairs," Myra said, as she stared James down. "As for you, I wish you had waited until he told us who the third person was before you killed him. Anyway, let's go say hi," Myra said as Maxwell and James started following her to the elevator.

James stopped. "Oh shit! I just realized I forgot something in my room. You guys go ahead of me and I'll join you in a few seconds," James said as he ran the other direction.   Maxwell turned to go after him when Myra stopped him.

"Don't worry. He'll come."

"How do you know?"

"Because if he decided to desert us now, that would mean that I have failed."

"So, because you're always right, is how you know," Maxwell said as he got in the elevator.

"Because I can't be wrong that many times," she said as the door closed.

Chapter 27

Luther smashed in the front door as Alice and Michelle strolled into the compound.

"Wow! Talk about a welcome party." Michelle grinned.

"Huh, she did realize that we were coming," Luther said, surprised.

Alice reached for her gun, but she was stopped by Michelle.

"Nah, this is my time!" she said to Alice. She turned to face Myra's followers. "Hi, sorry about breaking the door. I'm Michelle and this is my brother Luther. We just want to make sure we all have fun today." Michelle ended that sentence with an uncanny smile as she and Luther walked toward them.

Myra's followers were so shocked by how brazen the two of them seemed that they hesitated to attack. The duo had killed one of their own and just walked over the homeless man's dead body like he was nothing. That action itself sent them flying in a fit of rage as they attacked Michelle and Luther.

Blood was flying all over the place, and it was obvious that they both were toying around with Myra's followers. With every punch that Michelle landed, a stream of blood followed. Luther used the metal pipe. With every swing, the blood flowed like rain. A drop fell on Alice's cheek. Alice was in a trance as she watched those two decimate their enemies. She couldn't help but close her eyes and remember when she was in the army and met a Nova for the first time. Her whole squadron was destroyed by two Novas, and the only reason she survived was because an old man was passing by and rescued her. This time, the old man wasn't coming to the rescue. She steeled herself. She didn't need rescuing this time. Alice, with her chest held high, walked forward, stepping over bodies until it was over.

Michelle covered her mouth and nose with her bloody hands and inhaled, closing her eyes as she felt electricity run through her brain.

"Ahhh, that's what it's all about." She took her hands off, leaving a streak of blood around her mouth.

"You got a little something on your face," Luther said as he dropped the dented pipe on the floor.

"I should be arresting you." Alice joined them.

"Do you want to try?"

"Maybe if it was one on one."

Luther glared at Alice. "Do you want to repeat that again?"

"I said maybe if it was one on one!" Alice raised her voice.

Luther was about to attack Alice when Michelle barked, "Mother said no!" causing him to stop in his tracks.

Michelle got close to Alice's face. "When James is about to deliver the finishing blow, I will stop him, and I will break you into tiny pieces," she said with an eerie smile.

"That's if he can kill me. Otherwise, you can't touch me," Alice said.

The elevator dinged and all three of them glared at it, waiting for more followers to come out. Instead, Myra and Maxwell emerged.

When Alice laid her eyes on Myra, she clenched her fists and let out a scream as she rushed toward her in a fit of rage. Myra easily kicked her away.

"I trusted you!"

"You were meant to," Myra replied, without showing any expression.

"Was killing my husband part of your plan?" Alice asked as she clenched her fist, only to be interrupted by Michelle.

"Should we hug? We haven't seen each other in a long time."

"I was thinking of killing the both of you instead."

"So rude! Don't you think so, Luther?" Michelle asked.

"There's no reason to interact with failures, especially the two of them."

"Failures? Is that what you consider our brothers and sisters that you've killed?" Maxwell asked.

"Honestly, it always bothered me when the both of you called us brothers and sisters." Luther snared.

"What do you mean?" Both Myra and Maxwell asked.

Michelle turned to Luther. "Mother said to keep that quiet."

"Keep what quiet?" Myra yelled, only to hear laughter coming from Alice.

"So, this is how you look when you don't know the answers? That's not a pretty face," Alice said mockingly.

Myra recomposed herself. "So, we are here to kill each other, but why bring that thing here? Do you think it would sway me?"

"We brought her here on Mother's command."

"You expect me to believe that Mother is interested in a Lesser like her." Maxwell smirked at the idea.

"Mother is interested in her! After all we did to get her attention. The one she noticed was her!" Myra said. She growled at Alice and started walking toward her before hearing the elevator.

"She's mine," James said as he came out, dragging Marc behind him, with Elaine following.

"Marc!" Alice called out to him.

Maxwell dashed to Elaine's side. "I told you to stay down!"

"And I told you that I would always be next to you," Elaine responded. She gasped at the sight of her dead friends, but she couldn't look away; this was the road she had taken.

"I didn't want you to see this," Maxwell said.

"What the hell is wrong with you? Why are you treating her like one of us?" Luther snapped at Maxwell.

"Luther, calm down. Our brother can do whatever he pleases. He is under my protection." Myra stepped up to defend Maxwell. *Do you think I will let you sow distrust now, after all the work I did?* She thought.

James stepped forward standing opposite to Alice. "Let's do what we came here for!" James tried to snap

Marc's neck but was stopped by Alice's gun. James threw Marc to the side and dodged her bullets. They finally entered each other's range. Alice threw her empty gun at James as they started fighting each other. Every single one of James's attacks could have easily broken her bones. Just a brush to her skin left a burning sensation, but there was no fear in her eyes. She was like a reverse hurricane, calm and collected on the outside, but on the inside, a raging flame constantly thinking of ways to kill him.

The energy of the room changed as they all watched Alice stand up to James, everyone shocked except for Myra. She had sparred with Alice; by now, she knew what Alice was capable of more than anyone.

"Let's go upstairs and leave them to their fun," Myra said as she led everyone upstairs, leaving James and Alice.

As they walked up the empty staircase Michelle broke the silence. "Why did you stand up to us that day?"

"What do you mean?" Myra asked.

"We all knew the order of things except for you."

Myra stopped for a few seconds. *James might actually lose.* She thought before continuing. "I guess none of you did, because I'm supposed to be at the top," Myra said as they left the staircase.

Michelle let out a maniacal laugh. "Those are some big words from the invisible."

"I cease being invisible that day during the hunt," Myra replied.

"Funny, because you are seeing us now." Maxwell smirked.

"Oh crap, I forgot you were still here," Michelle said, looking surprised. "I thought you left already. What are you still doing here?" she said, antagonizing Maxwell.

"I see you guys learned how to talk crap over the years." Maxwell got angry.

"Mother instructed us to let you go," Luther said to Maxwell.

"Don't listen to them!" Myra interrupted as she dashed towards Michelle.

"You don't need to tell me twice," Maxwell said as he followed Myra's lead and clashed with Luther.

On the first floor, only a few minutes had passed, and Alice was completely bruised from James's attack brushing her. Marc had finally regained consciousness, but all he could do was watch as Alice fought James. He had lost all hope, but seeing Alice brought it back.

"You got this, sis!" he yelled trying to cheer her on.

"I guess I should have broken his jaw, but if I had done that, I wouldn't be able to hear him scream in pain like your husband," James said, as he try to attacked Alice repeatedly.

Alice kept dodging, attacking when she had the chance. James just brushed off her attacks like they were nothing to him. He was getting annoyed by how slippery Alice was, but he knew it wouldn't be long until he hit her. He needed just one hit—and finally, an opportunity came. Both Alice and James went for a straight punch, but James had the upper hand since he had started a split second before Alice. James could see everything, he could see his fist cross Alice's, but out of nowhere her fist sped up and landed squarely on his face, sending him falling on his ass. James was in shock. It was the first time that he had been brought to his ass by a Lesser. He quickly tried to get up, but all he saw was a blur and fell back again screaming in pain. Alice had taken his left eye.

"I told you I would make you suffer before I kill you. So, get up."

"Even I didn't cry like that!" Marc yelled from the side.

Alice looked at Marc, feeling horrible, because she was the reason he got tortured.

"Take your time. Seeing him get his ass kick is healing me!" Marc yelled, causing Alice to smile, but she quickly saw the look on Marc's face change. Alice swiftly took half a step back and saw James's fist fly in front of her. She easily countered him, leaving his face bloody, but James didn't let that stop him. He couldn't understand what was happening; she became faster than before and for a second, she disappeared to his blind side, and he saw half of the world turn sideways as he fell to the ground. He tried to get back up but fell forward.

"What did you do to me?"

Alice pulled out another gun and fired twice at James's kneecaps. For the first time in his life, James felt that his life was in danger, and fear overcame him as he tried to crawl away from her. Alice stomped on his injured knee. "Where are you going?"

"Wait, wait! If you let me go, my brothers and sisters will spare you."

"Funny, because two of them told me if I didn't kill you, they would kill me."

"You're nothing!" James lost it.

Bang! Bang! Alice fired two more shots, one at each of his hands, then another two at his elbow with a smile on her face.

"Well, that makes two Nova wannabes down."
Alice laughed maniacally as she put her gun on James's
head and left it there for a couple of seconds until she was
sure that he could feel the cold piece on his skin and finally
pulled the trigger.

Click! "I guess I'm out of ammo." She giggled at
the sight of James sweating in fear.
"Don't worry I brought extra." She pulled out one bullet out
of her pocket and loaded it.

"Any last words?"

James knew he was going to die. "What does that
make you?" he snarled.

Alice hesitated, looked at Marc, who was barely
holding on, and lowered her gun. "I don't have time to deal
with you." She walked past James, leaving him with a
sense of hope. James sighed as if he was holding on to the
whole world.

Bang! A bullet pierced James's head, leaving him
gushing in a pool of blood.

"That makes me better than you. I don't care
anymore, and nothing will stop me from getting my
revenge." She dropped her gun on the ground and rushed to
Marc's side, helping him get up.

"I'm sorry it took so long."

"Why are you apologizing? I was able to see you kick his ass. What more could I want?" Marc said as he leaned on Alice.

"I used you to bring him out."

"I figured as much when I saw you." He smiled.

"Why are you smiling?"

"It'll take a month at the most for me to be back to my young self, but… Anyway, what's a couple of broken bones for family." Marc smiled.

"Richard is lucky to have you in his life."

"We are lucky to be in each other's lives. In many ways if it wasn't for Richard, I probably wouldn't survive this," Marc said before passing out again.

"Marc, Marc! Shit I need to get him to the car as soon as possible," she said as she carried Marc's limp body out of the factory.

As they were walking out, Alice stopped in her tracks as she saw a man walk in reading a book in one hand and had his other hand in his pocket. She had seen him multiple times on tv, but seeing him in person was different.

"Darius." Alice blurred out from shock, trembling in fear at the sight of the man.

The man stopped as he got close to her. "How's the old man doing?" he asked, still looking at his book. She instantly knew who he was asking about.

"I haven't seen him in years," Alice answered as her heart started racing.

"It's a shame that you're not even worth my time," the man said as he went inside the factory.

Alice rushed to get Marc in her car and sat behind the wheel. Her hands shook from her interaction with Darius. She drove away from the scene to get Marc to a hospital.

On the second floor, the four of them were fighting. Myra had the advantage in her fight against Michelle and so did Maxwell against Luther.

"Do you mind if I join?" Darius's voice echoed into the room, stopping everyone in their tracks and turning their attention to him. A moment of shock spread on their faces as they realized who was standing in front of them.

"No, it can't be," Myra said. Maxwell stepped back, getting closer to Elaine.

Luther and Michelle started laughing.

"I get first dibs," Luther said as he started walking toward Darius.

"I would recommend you all to come at me," Darius said as he kept reading his book.

Luther rushed toward Darius, wanting to test his mettle against the so-called strongest man.

In a split second, everyone in the room was speechless as they watched Darius snap Luther's head backward with one hand, still reading his book, killing him in one motion.

Michelle backed away as Darius got closer. Finally, he closed his book and looked at them.

"You must be Myra," he said, looking at Elaine.

"That would be me." Myra stepped forward.

"Oh, it's hard to tell you guys apart."

"Are you working for Mother?"

"I have an agreement with the one you call Mother," Darius said as he kept walking toward Myra.

"He was on your side, and you killed him!" Michelle said in anger.

"You're still alive, aren't you? Unless you want me to change that."

Michelle stepped back at the risk of losing her life. "So, what are you doing here?"

Now Darius stood face to face with Myra holding his book in one hand. "I'm here to take care of her thorn," he said nonchalantly.

Myra realized that she was in danger and swiftly attacked him multiple times which he easily parried, looking bored.

"I was expecting more from this thorn," Darius said as Myra's vision dimmed and she fell forward. He had knocked her out with one quick jab.

"You can take her to your boss," Darius said to Michelle. He opened his book and made his way to Maxwell.

"What's going to happen to her?" Maxwell asked Darius, who just put his finger up, signaling him to wait as he kept reading. Michelle carried Myra out the building.

Finally, he finished the book. "Have you ever read *'When God Cried'*?"

Maxwell stood in front of Elaine in a defensive position. "What do you want?"

"Not to be hubristic, but every time I read this book, I can't help but feel his pain. God in his loneliness created humans in his image and gave them free will so that they would one day evolve to become new gods, and he would finally have someone to talk to. After thousands of years, a human finally evolved into a new god, which brought the old God so much happiness; he now had someone to talk to. And can you guess what happened next?" Darius said, pacing back and forth.

"The new God killed the old one because the last part of his evolution to a new god was seeing humanity's history from beginning to the end, which was him. The creation of a new God required the life of every other human, since the old God wanted only one companion. Full of rage, the new God killed the old God," Maxwell replied.

"And the old God shed a tear for the first time in his life as he died. Do you know why?"

"Because he didn't get his wish."

"On the contrary, he cried because he was happy that his wish came true. He could see the future. He knew he would die but for those few seconds, he could see his reflection in someone else's eyes, and that was worth it." Darius faced Maxwell. "Well anyway, let's get back to business."

"So, you're going to tell me why you are here?"

"I'm here to decide whether you live or die."

"I was worried you might say that, but can you let her go?"

"No! I'm not leaving." Elaine said as she grabbed Maxwell's arm.

"I think you'll fight better if you have someone to protect," Said Darius.

"I'll fight you. Just let her go."

"I'm not known for changing my mind. I'll give you thirty seconds to attack me before I start." Darius started counting out loud.

Some of Maxwell's hits would land and others would miss, but Darius never stopped counting. With every hit that Maxwell landed, he started to lose hope as his fist started hurting. Darius's hard muscles acted like a shield, protecting him from Maxwell's attack.

"27,28,29,30." As soon as he was done counting, he landed one attack on Maxwell and dropped him to the ground. "Disappointing."

Elaine ran toward him to help him up his feet, only to be stopped by Darius.

"In this world there's only one person that I love, and I would do anything to keep her safe. That is my weakness and strength. It is only through loss that you can know your limit. So, let's see how much he loves you," Darius said as he started squeezing her arm.

Hearing Elaine scream, Maxwell grabbed Darius's leg, swung him into a broken piece of furniture, and rushed to Elaine.

"Are you ok?"

"Yes." She answered.

Maxwell knew that this was not over. "You need to leave now."

"I'm not leaving without you," she exclaimed.

"I can't beat him if I'm worried about you. As soon as I'm done, I'll meet you at our cabin," he whispered to her.

"There's no escape, unless you can kill me," Darius said as he brushed off the dust from his jacket.

"Run!" Maxwell yelled, as he attacked Darius, giving Elaine the chance to escape.

Darius grabbed his fists. "You're going to have to do better than that."

"I think I'm doing really good against the strongest human on the planet," Maxwell said with a smirk.

"Why do you think that?" Darius said, bringing Maxwell to his knee.

"I don't need to defeat you; I just need to buy time."

Darius started laughing. "Let me show you why I'm the strongest," he said, releasing his grip on Maxwell. He landed multiple hits on him, before dropping him for a second time, bloody on the floor. Darius grabbed Maxwell by the arm and dragged him to the window. He lifted him up and threw him out. Maxwell was strong and normally could have handled that fall, but he was in poor condition and took the full blow of the fall right as Elaine came out of the factory, screaming at the horror. She saw the man that she loved bloody on the ground and rushed to his side.

Darius jumped from the second floor. "I really wanted you to be a success, to be the one that could kill me, to see my reflection in your eyes…Time to die," he said.

Maxwell struggled to get up, his body in unimaginable pain. Tears rolled down Elaine's cheeks. "It seems that it's my turn to buy you time," she said as she faced Darius.

"No! Get out of here! Please!"

"How can I?" she said as she attacked Darius. Every hit she landed on him left her fist bloody and Darius unfazed. It was like hitting a wall.

"Please, please! Let her go!" Maxwell yelled. He used all his strength to get up, only for his legs to give. He punched his own leg. "No! I'm better than this!"

"You are courageous," Darius said, as Elaine kept attacking him. "But courage without power is useless." He snapped her head, and Maxwell watched the woman he loved fall. Maxwell grabbed her before she hit the ground. "No, no, no, no, please wake up," he said, desperately tapping her cheeks without any response. He just wanted to hear her voice one more time. He pulled her dead body close.

"I'm sorry. I'm so sorry. Please say something," he cried in her ear.

Darius watched Maxwell break in front of him. "Are you done?"

As quickly as sadness had come over Maxwell, so did rage. He laid Elaine down and faced Darius. He'd never been that angry before. He felt like the rage was suffocating him, like he was going to explode. That's when Darius saw Maxwell's eyes change into a blue and red color, like a Nova.

"I guess you weren't a failure after all, let's-" Before he could finish that sentence, Maxwell's fist crushed through the iron muscle and pushed Darius back. All the pain was gone, replaced with rage. A rage that his body couldn't communicate. His attack was never strong enough. He wanted to shatter every bone; he wanted to break Darius. Until he finally sent him flying to the ground.

Darius got up. He could taste his blood for the first time in a long time. He wiped the dripping blood from his mouth and looked at it.

"You pass," he said, relieved.

Maxwell attacked him again, but this time Darius showed him why he was called the strongest, as he crushed him to the ground and pummeled him until he passed out.

He picked up the passed-out Maxwell and flung him over his shoulder. He looked back at Elaine's dead body.

"Thank you for taking care of my son. I feel like I should give you a burial, but my son won't remember you. So, here," he said. He pulled his book out of his jacket, threw it on her dead body and left with Maxwell.

<u>'When God cried'</u>

Chapter 28

Alice sat in the hospital's waiting room, anticipating the results of Marc's surgery.

Richard rushed in and saw Alice. "Where is he?"

"He's inside. the doctor is trying to save his hand."

"What did you do?" Richard yelled.

"Sir, I'm going to ask you to keep it down or leave," the nurse said, trying to defuse the situation.

"The man that I love is hurt because of her. Don't ask me to calm down!"

"Look around you. Everyone that's here is here because they or their loved ones are hurt, but you don't see them screaming. Do you know why? Because that won't help. You're only making everyone around you more worried. Your friend here was the one that brought him in. She was the one who helped him, and I would take a guess that she was the one that called you. So why don't you take a seat and wait with your friend here?" the nurse said. Richard took a seat next to Alice as the nurse went back to her work.

"I'm mad at you," Richard said after a couple minutes of silence.

"I don't blame you."

"You know what's the worst part? I'm not mad at you because Marc got hurt. I'm mad that my partner went behind my back after I told her no…"

"I did what needed to be done."

"Did you even get him?"

"I did. I killed him."

"How do you feel?"

"Still angry. Knowing that he's dead gives me some relief. At the same time, the rage in me is refueled, because there is one more person I need to kill."

"Are you even listening to yourself? You are not the judge, jury, and executioner."

"Why shouldn't I be? It happened to me! I should get to decide and no one else!"

The nurse cleared her throat loudly.

"When you lost Phillip, I didn't know what to say. I knew you were still investigating James and knew that you wanted to kill him, but who was I to stop you? But I should have stopped you just like I did now."

"What did you do?"

"I have some officers waiting outside to take you in. But I talked to the chief, and we agreed that if you decide to run, we won't pursue you."

Alice laughed "Escape. You know me too well for that. You didn't do anything wrong," she said as she got up.

"Wait...Phillip's funeral is this Saturday."

"I guess I'll see you then. Marc is an amazing man that truly loves you. So, what are you waiting for?"

"For him to wake up," Richard said as he pulled out an engagement box.

"Don't forget to invite me to the wedding," Alice said as she headed toward the officers waiting outside to arrest her.

"Fool, who else could be my maid of honor?" Richard whispered.

The officers didn't handcuff her; they just drove her to the precinct, walked her to the chief's office, and left.

"So, I sent some officers to check out the scene. There was nothing when they got there," said the Chief.

"I didn't think they would work that fast."

"Which means I can't charge you with anything, unless Marc decides to press charges against you."

"He should. Someone like me cannot be out in the world. I have so much rage in me."

"You seem to be handling it well."

"What the hell is handling it well? Putting your friend at risk? Watching as a bunch of people get slaughtered and doing nothing?" Alice clenched her jaw.

"You're one of my best, and I've never seen you like this. I don't think this is how Phillip would like to see you."

"I guess I should go back to how everything used to be and hope for rainbows and butterflies. Every time I close my eyes, I can see him. I just found out who was the mastermind behind that night, and you expect me to just go back to normal?" Alice said as he pulled out her gun and badge.

"Do you know what you are doing?" the chief asked.

"Why should someone else decide my justice?"

"Because you're not seeing things right. You need help."

Alice handed her gun and badge and resigned.

A couple of miles away, a woman was working on her computer when Darius walked in.

"How was he?" the woman asked while working.

"I haven't bled in a long time."

"So, it was a success?"

"You're still alive, aren't you? What's so special about that girl?" Darius questioned.

"She wanted to kill me, so I have to re-educate her," the woman said as she turned around revealing her metallic irises. She grabbed a small suitcase next to her and kicked it to him.

"Can you not show me those eyes?"

The woman closed her eyes and opened them, revealing hazel irises. She closed them a second time and revealed her metallic irises again, taunting him.

"Open the suitcase. It's a gift for bringing her alive."

Darius opened the suitcase and saw a small container with a metallic liquid inside.

"What is this?"

"The cure."

"What's the cost?"

"Five days. Once used, the person will die after five days, two hours, and ten minutes."

"That's more than enough," Darius said. He was about to close the suitcase when a second compartment revealed a dark ball which, upon Darius's touch, started glowing dark blue and floated into the air. "What is this?"

"I couldn't figure out what kind of weapon to give the strongest man on this planet, so I figured, why not all of them? Just think of a weapon."

Darius thought and saw the ball morph into a spear. "Too slow," he said as he grabbed it.

"Don't worry, the more you use it, the quicker the response will be. It will know your fighting and will learn to know what you need before you even know it. It will become second nature to you."

The spear morphed around his hand and turned into a bracelet. "I guess it'll do," he said as he left.

Once Darius left, she got off her computer and stood in the middle of her room.

"Lab six," she said, as a circular light formed around her. It took her down like an elevator until she got to her destination. Her phone rang.

"I had a feeling you would be calling," she said as she walked.

"How did it go?" an altered voice came through.

"Well, I am about to move to phase two."

"Good."

"I will be incorporating a new subject to test the N2 gene."

"I look forward to hearing the results," the voice said as they hung up.

Mother's eyes changed to a hazel color as she walked into a white room with Myra cuffed on a table.

"You seem very calm."

"Why shouldn't I be? You trained me to be calm minded in any situation. Don't you remember?" Myra said.

"Apparently, I did too great a job at that. You weren't able to awaken."

"What do you mean 'awaken?'"

"Nothing you need to know."

"Since you're not going to kill me, I have a question to ask."

"Who said I'm not planning on killing you?"

"You would have done it by now."

"Ask your question."

"What did Luther mean when he said it bothered him when Maxwell and I called him brother?"

"Maybe because you both used to be weaker than them."

"Funny, I am the one being restrained but you're the one lying."

Mother walked next to Myra and started taking a seat as the floor moved and formed into a chair out of thin air.

"Nanobots?" asked Myra.

"The whole building. And they're all connected here," she said, as she pointed at her temple.

"So, you are a Teltius."

Mother blinked and revealed metallic eyes. "Does that answer your question?"

"Not the first question I asked."

"The others were created in pods, to make you stronger. You and Maxwell were born the old-fashioned way."

"So, I have real parents? Hmm. I thought I would be more moved about this."

"That's the problem."

"What?"

"You're too much like me. But it's fine, we'll fix that," Mother said, as two electrical spikes came out of the table and stabbed Myra's temples, sending a piercing scream throughout the room. Mother got up to leave. "Time to go recruit my new subject."

Chapter 29

"My husband has always stood up for what he thought was right. He was a professor who always went the extra mile for his students. He believed that changing the future for the better isn't just fighting for change now, but also teaching the younger generation what change looks like. I watched his last moments. He was strong until the end. Seeing everyone here right now is proof of how amazing he was," Alice said as she stood in front of a large group of officers and students that had come to say goodbye to Phillip.

After burying Phillip, Marc and Richard went to talk to Alice. "You know you can always move back in with us," Marc said.

"I know. I just need some time to myself. How's your hand and leg?"

"He'll be back to normal after a month. The doctor said the biggest thing was the blood loss," Richard answered.

Alice grabbed both of their hands. "I'm really sorry for dragging you into this."

"I'm your partner. I wish you would have talked to me. I wish you would talk to me." Richard growled.

"Richard, stop it. I'm fine. Thank you for being here for him," Alice said, as she stepped away from them. "Congrats on the engagement."

"Hello. You must be Alice?" Neveah walked up to Alice.

"Thank you for coming."

"Of course. I only knew him for a short time, but he was an amazing person. It is because of him that I'm Mayor."

"Now that you're the new mayor, you better make him proud."

"I plan on it. If you need anything, just reach out to my office," Neveah said, as her security signaled her that it was time to go. "Sorry about this. It's been non-stop."

"Just make us proud," Alice said as she watched everyone leave.

The seats were being taken away when Michelle came and sat behind her. "Did you miss me?"

"Is Myra alive?"

"Do you want to know?"

"Is she?"

"I don't know, but the person who does would like to meet you."

"This mother person."

"So, do you want to come?"

Alice took a second to look at her dead husband's grave. "Let's go."

Michelle drove her to a building and guided her in.

"I'm surprised you're still alive. I saw him go in the facility," said Alice.

"Darius killed my brother, and there was nothing I could do."

"So, you know how I feel," Alice snarled.

"I guess I do. You know, we were made to feel special from a young age but finding out that we aren't as special as we thought was shocking, to say the least."

"Sound like you got what you deserve."

"Maybe," Michelle answered as she stopped in front of a big door. "She is waiting inside."

Alice walked in and saw a woman working on a cadaver lying on a table. As she got closer, she saw that it was James.

"You did a great job dealing with him. The old man taught you well."

"Excuse me?"

Mother turned and looked at Alice for the first time, revealing her metallic irises.

"You're a Teltius. Why am I not surprised?"

"The way you took James down, is one of the few ways to take a Nova down. Attacking his joints to slow him down and when that happened, attacking his weak point. For you, that was his eyes and ear. There's only one man alive with a similar fighting style."

"So, you know him?"

"I try to know the relevant people."

"I'm guessing that I'm relevant since I'm here."

Mother stepped away from the body as it sank into the floor and disappeared "I'm guessing you're looking for Myra." Two chairs formed from the floor and she sat down.

Alice took a seat. "I am."

"Do you think you could kill her?"

"Yes."

Mother smirked. "Maybe if he had finished training

you completely, there would have been a chance but as you are now, your chance of beating her would be 2.34%."

"Sounds like I have a chance."

"What if I told you I could increase that chance to fifty percent?"

"How?"

"I could turn you into an EVO."

"What's an EVO?"

"The next evolution of humanity. That's what Myra is."

"Would I become a killer like her?"

"You don't have to kill if you don't want to."

"So, what's the side effect?"

"None. Just super strength and speed. Basically, you'll be as strong as a Nova."

"Didn't Ethan lose to a Nova?"

"He fought against a trained Nova after he had just sat on his ass for years. The result was obvious. You, on the other hand, have been training your whole life. Imagine what you could do. You would never feel powerless again."

"Instead of that, why don't you just hand Myra over to me, and I can take care of her."

"I would love to, but she escaped from us."

"What?" Alice got off her seat.

"Yeah, I turned my back on her for a second and

she disappeared."

"You know what she's capable of doing. You have all this information at your fingertips--can't you find her?"

"She's also Myra. If she doesn't want to be found, she won't be."

"So, what's the point of this?!"

"Well, given time, I will find her, but the question is: Will you be part of the recovery team?"

Alice thought about it. "If I do this, I will be able to kill her."

"Yes."

"Let's do it. By the way, what should I call you?"

"Akila," Mother said before Alice's chair sealed her.

"What's going on?" She yelled before being stabbed multiple times through her back and feeling a burning sensation inside her body.

Akila got off her chair, made her way to her computer. She pulled up a screen showing an image of a body and Alice's name on top. She located 'N2' on the screen, pressed it and watched as green spread throughout Alice's image.

Thank you Vanna the eyeball doctor for helping me make this happen.

Printed in Great Britain
by Amazon

10922411R00205